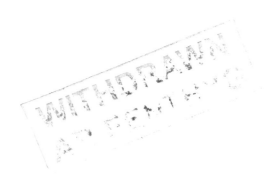

Cody's Fight

Mel Cody travelled over a thousand miles to visit his father's Arizona homeland, but upon his arrival he is forced to intervene when local thugs cruelly set upon an old man in the street. The area's most powerful rancher, Casper Spool, does not appreciate Cody's interference and they become mutual enemies.

So, when Rebecca Church arrives in town, intending to work a rundown plot of inherited land, and puts a stumbling block in the path of Spool's ruthless advance across the territory, both Mel and Rebecca must join forces and fight their common enemy. But with the odds stacked against them, can they overcome Spool and his cronies whilst protecting the land, and each other?

Cody's Fight

Caleb Rand

A Black Horse Western

ROBERT HALE · LONDON

© Caleb Rand 2012
First published in Great Britain 2012

ISBN 978-0-7198-0580-6

Robert Hale Limited
Clerkenwell House
Clerkenwell Green
London EC1R 0HT

www.halebooks.com

Typeset by
Derek Doyle & Associates, Shaw Heath
Printed and bound in Great Britain by
CPI Antony Rowe, Chippenham and Eastbourne

1

Midway between Phoenix, Arizona and the Colorado River, the town of Polvo Gris was circled by hills that trapped heat and dust. The town had sprung up near the lower slopes of the Eagle Tail Mountains, not far from the timber-stands of pine and spruce from which some local folk gleaned a living.

Where dense agave and mescal filtered the breezes that would have otherwise brought relief to the bleak settlement, Melvin Cody's horse shifted anxiously under him. He checked it and held it quiet while he spared a thought for his father.

It was twenty-five years since a young and adventurous Hammond Cody had heard tell of the immense, bountiful territories that lay far to the north. From Polvo Gris, he'd travelled a thousand miles to the Canadian border. In Moose Jaw, he'd traded his cow pony and pack mule for a canoe and traps, paddled the Qu'Appelle until he made it to

5

the shores of the Quill Lakes. That was near to where he'd meet Morning Sky, the Cree chieftain's daughter he'd later marry, who was to become Melvin's mother.

Melvin leaned forward and patted the neck of his mare, then recalled the cheerless, dying words of his father. 'The company men ... the fur traders are moving in, son. There's no room for the buckskinner any more. You *ain't* got your ma, so just go. If you ever make it back, take your time. Look over the country about – look in any direction. Make it *your* country.'

So now Mel Cody *had* arrived here fully grown, and years later than he should have – perhaps too late to make any part of it his own country. The mare shifted again, impatient to get moving, wearied by the heat and another day's ride. She wanted water and feed. Mel gave her free rein, and she ambled toward the rough trail that led to Polvo Gris.

Horse and rider flickered in the heat-shimmer off the land. The horse was an iron-grey quarter horse, well-built. Despite her weariness she was sure of foot. Mel was tall and slim, and rode at ease in the saddle. He had the sun burned skin of a mixed-blood and his dark, deep-set eyes looked around with the confidence of a man who'd seen much. He travelled in a mail-order black suit. He knew it would be uncomfortable, but he'd decided that's what you probably wore if and when you travelled beyond Flat Stone.

6

Two miles out from Polvo Gris, Mel let his horse pick a solitary trail. When he finally rode into the town, he kept to the west side of the main street, where there was shade from the slanting sun. The grey nickered and crow-hopped excitedly on smelling the water in a nearby street trough. Mel let her go for the water.

Two townsmen walked across the street toward him. Mel nodded civilly. 'Where can I get my horse taken care of?'

'Livery. Turn left past Marcella's. That's the place we go to drink, and there ain't no choice,' one of the men said bluntly.

Mel said thanks, unsure of who or what 'no choice' applied to. He drew his horse from the tepid water and walked on, clasping one hand to the horn of his saddle. With his hat brim bent low, he looked along the main street. He glanced indifferently at the paint-peeled store fronts and bleached boardwalks, the overall dried-out decay. He passed Marcella's Quarter and considered buying a drink. He had little idea of how long he'd be staying in Polvo Gris or what it had to offer. Maybe he'd go back to the saloon a little later, after he'd taken care of his horse.

On the side of a building, an arrow pointed down a side street. Under it was a sign that read: FRATER'S LIVERY STABLE.

Mel turned down the muck-covered lane. With his usual caution, he pressed the palm of his left hand into the butt of his gun, a .44 Colt tucked snugly in the beaded sash around his waist.

The town was quiet in this near-to-noon hour, with only a small number of people on the move. But when Mel was in sight of the open doors of the livery stable, someone staggered in front of him. From one side of the street, Selwyn Church wavered then stopped, lurched forward and fell to his knees.

Church was an elder, with enough years to be venerated by a mixed-blood Cree. He was cowering, his pale eyes burning with fear.

A gun fired, roared twice in the narrowness of the street. The bullets buried themselves in the ground either side of the old man's knees and kept him from moving.

Mel pulled on his horse's mane and made some comforting sounds. He twisted slightly in the saddle as four men appeared from a pole-fronted stable yard. One stepped forward challengingly; two others held back. The fourth clung tightly to the halter of a bad-tempered chestnut gelding, trying to soothe it.

Budge Miner took a brief look at Mel. The man was big, but he hesitated a moment before waving Mel away. Then he smiled coldly, pulled back his fist and piled his knuckles down hard into the back of the man's neck.

Church didn't make a sound – just went down with his face driven hard into the dung-encrusted ground. He did cry out when Miner kicked him in the legs, ribs, and the side of his head.

But it wasn't Mel's affair. It wasn't like it was his town, and he didn't have his bearings. 'Why don't you leave the old feller alone?' he asked, uneasily. 'Looks to me like he's had enough.'

Miner waited while Mel's words sank in, then he turned on his heel. He bunched his fist and blew on his knuckles. 'Back off,' he threatened.

As Mel spared a quick look at the other two, Miner reached down and pulled Church from the dust. He held him with one hand and slapped his face with the other.

Mel, shaken, touched his horse's belly with his boot heels and the animal lunged forward. He swung the grey to the left and the horse's shoulder smashed the tall man away.

Mel swung from the saddle and danced forward quickly. His right hand gripped Miner's, his left positioned low into his midriff. The blow exploded the man's breath away, staggered him a step or two backwards. Mel turned quickly to see the expected advance of the other two men.

His left hand moved quickly to his waistband, drew his Colt. The two men stopped in their tracks. One was eyeing the big man behind Mel. Mel turned to find the man had drawn his own gun halfway from its holster. 'That'd be real stupid. Me with my gun already pointed at your gut an' all.'

Church staggered to his feet and stood, wheezing

and watching. He took a step back against a building. Then he pushed himself away from the wall, and drew his own gun.

His eyes were rheumy, but hate-filled when he pulled the trigger. His bony wrist bucked and the bullet whistled high above and between the two other men. They cursed in unison and stared hard at Mel. But then the man who'd been holding the fractious gelding dropped its headstall, drew a pistol from his belt and fired in one violent movement.

Church dropped his gun and clutched his knotty fingers to his shirt front. He let out a whisper of air, twisted futilely at his darkening shirtfront.

He sniffed at the air and smiled. But he wasn't smiling – he was saying something, grimacing as pain coursed through his gaunt frame. He was dying, crumpling to the ground, when Mel's shot ripped the horse minder's arm apart, sent the gelding rearing and bucking away down the side street.

'I never done them no harm . . . never stole cattle,' the old man croaked. Then his dry lips ceased to move against the hard-packed dirt. His legs jerked once, then he died.

Mel grabbed the big man roughly, hurled him at his two companions. He raised his Colt and set the action.

The big man rasped loudly. 'In hell's name, mister, I don't know who you are, but you just bought yourself a real load of trouble.'

'Someone sure did.' Mel looked past the men as someone turned into the side street. This man was different, though. He carried a shotgun, and wore a star on the lapel of his short hickory coat.

2

Sheriff Brett Vaughn walked fast, taking notice of the stricken old man. He stopped just short of Mel, eyed him with professional judgement, then spoke to the big man. 'Budge Miner ... I might have known. Speak to me, and make it good.'

The big man glared furiously at the lawman for a moment before he answered. 'This weren't my play, Sheriff. We came in here after a damned cattle thief, an' we caught us one. It was Selwyn Church – him and this fellow here.'

Vaughn looked sidelong at Church's pathetic body. He spat drily and cursed.

'Make sure you aim your spitting an' cursing right.' Miner pointed at Mel. 'Him an' Church stole some of Casper Spool's stock ... hid 'em up on Church's place. We followed their tracks into town. I figure they were planning for the stock auction: there'll be enough of them Phoenix buyers here.

They ain't too watchful about the brands they're buying. *You* know that, Sheriff.'

Vaughn looked cautiously at Mel. 'Well?'

'I don't know what they're talking about,' Mel retorted. 'I do know the big plug-ugly here's a liar. But I've never seen any o' the others before, an' that's the truth.'

'How'd you get involved?' the sheriff asked.

'I just rode in ... was following the livery stable sign. They came out ... started bulldogging the old feller. He drew his gun all right, but he was beaten so bad he couldn't see proper. They weren't good odds, Sheriff. The one there with half an arm's a killer.'

Vaughn turned his attention to the man Mel indicated. 'What you got to say, Rourke? Is what he says right?'

Rourke was holding his shattered arm tight against his chest. Pain distorted his face and drained him of colour.

'I need a doctor,' he groaned. 'Budge told it right. They must have been stealing Spool's cattle. Church went for his gun. I had to shoot. Now someone get me to McLane.'

'You heard him. So get the 'breed in your jail, Sheriff,' Miner said, still breathing hard. 'An' you keep him there 'til Mr Spool comes to take a look at him. Them tracks tell their own tale.'

Vaughn threw a worried look in Mel's direction. 'You keep your big mouth to yourself, Budge, else I'll

walk away and leave you to sort it out amongst yourselves. You really want that?'

But for the moment, Miner had the protection of
a county sheriff. 'You know how Mr Spool deals with
cattle thieves, Brett? If there ain't a cottonwood
handy, he'll drag 'em 'til their skin turns red.' With
that, he licked his lips at his dark humour and looked
hard at Mel.

Mel didn't like Miner's reference to his mixed
blood. His eyes turned black and bored through the
big man as he pushed his Colt back into his waistband.

Vaughn saw a look that told him Budge Miner was
a dead man if he didn't step in.

Reluctantly, Vaughn swung his shotgun at Mel. 'I
know what you're thinking, stranger. I'll take that
Colt if you don't mind.'

'What about *one-arm*?' Mel asked, even and slow.

'There ain't no doubt Selwyn drew a gun first.
Much as I'd like, I'm not holding Rourke for anything. Anyway, leave him standing much longer, and
he'll likely bleed to death.'

'I told you, Sheriff, I just rode in. I was looking to
get oats for the grey.'

The sheriff looked as though he was getting
bored. 'Yeah, that's as may be,' he said. 'But there's
this other matter of the stolen Spool cattle. I can't
just turn you loose an' you know it.' Vaughn drew
back the twin hammers of his shotgun. 'Now, last

time, hand over your gun.'

Mel took a short breath, then grumbled and huffed as he decided. He took a few steps toward the sheriff. 'You take it,' he said. 'I don't give it to no one. There's a difference.'

'Yeah, I just bet there is,' Vaughn said as he lifted the Colt and admired the glass-beaded waistband. 'What tribe's that?'

'Cree. My ma,' he added, knowing the sheriff was wondering.

'Well, that's a hell of a long ways off, son. I ain't ever been further north than Wolf Hole, myself,' Vaughn said with a half-smile.

Once Vaughn had Mel's gun, Miner grimaced sourly and his mouth started working again. 'Now we'll see if you've got a fork in your tongue, see how you holler when a loop of hemp starts squeezing your neck.'

'Get out of my way,' the sheriff snapped. 'Any of you men make a move I don't like, an' I'll blast your goddamn hides. This is a lawful take now, an' I'm handling it. You'll do best to get your stories off pat, 'cause I'm warning you now: if there's any lying been done, you'll find little comfort in this town from now on.'

Miner held up his hand in mock acceptance. 'We got 'em all but branded, Sheriff. You see if we ain't.'

Vaughn nudged Mel in the side and motioned for him to move on.

15

Mel held out his hand and waited for the grey to
come to him. He led the mare back to the main
street, muttering about having to wait for a rub down
and feed. He turned alongside the dry, grey boardwalk, and headed for the jailhouse. The small crowd
who'd gathered watched him in curious dumb
silence. One of them stepped forward and spat at his
feet and he stopped, but another nudge from
Vaughn made him go on.

Mel carefully hitched his horse outside the jailhouse while staring back down the street. He pushed
aside the half-open door and walked into the small,
heat-choked building. He gasped and wondered why
Vaughn had called it the cooler. Vaughn turned the
key in the first of three cells. He took off his sweat-
stained hat, cursed and wiped his gleaming
forehead. Standing at his desk, he flicked and
fumbled at some papers. 'Right here ain't the best
spot in town, mister. So you can start by telling me
what I don't already know. What's your name?'

'Melvin Cody.' Mel didn't think any sort of Cree
name would help him much in the circumstances, or
that now was the time to go *Injun*.

'How did you meet up with Selwyn Church?'

'I already told you, Sheriff. The one called Miner
was giving him a real beating. I suggested he leave
him alone. Said I thought he'd taken enough.'

16

'Seems a fair request. What happened then?'

'All four of 'em started to act real hostile. I think they wanted to kill the old'un all on their own. What was his name . . . Selwyn?'

'Yeah, Selwyn Church.' Vaughn looked hard at Mel. 'An' you never seen him before? You're sticking to that story?'

'I'm just sticking to the truth, Sheriff. I'm hoping you're going to do the same. I ain't taking any of your bootleg justice for something I ain't done.'

'It'll be the *truth* that gets its chance, mister,' the sheriff said with a wry smile. 'I know there are maybe others around here who'll tell it different, but right now you need a better excuse than taking your mount for a feed.'

Mel looked through the bars at the bleak, feature-less surroundings, remembered his pa telling him not to take much heed of them. 'I never did make the stable. Can you take care of my horse?'

Vaughn nodded.'Yeah, I'll get it done. Now, you just rode in, Melvin Cody, so maybe you can tell me where you been the last few days . . . up 'til this mornin?'

Mel's shoulders slumped and he groaned inwardly at his misfortune. For the last two weeks, he'd rode from Lake Powell and the Utah border and made lone camps. He'd seen a cattle drive trailing south along the Colorado River toward Yuma, but he'd spoken to no one since leaving Salt Lake City.

17

When Mel didn't give an immediate answer, Vaughn laid out the full details of the circumstances. 'If you haven't got a better answer, it don't improve matters. That outfit you just crossed? They're Spool men, an' Casper ain't exactly what you'd call a yearling, if you get my meaning. When Budge Miner tells him what happened here, he'll come down like a blue norther.'

Mel wanted to ask where the sheriff would be during all this but decided he was in deep enough, and held his tongue again. He stretched out on the grimy crib and realized he was badly placed. If Casper Spool was that powerful, how would Vaughn stack up against him, what back-up did he have? Mel didn't intend to be hanged, that was for sure. He was a fast learner, and hadn't let another man best him for many years.

Vaughn placed his shotgun on top of the papers. Then he pulled his revolver, checked the cylinder and holstered it. He opened the sand-blasted window, blinked at the hot dusty breeze.

Ten minutes later, two men delivered Selwyn Church's body to the jailhouse. Vaughn thanked them, then asked them to take Mel's grey to the stable and have it looked after.

With a great deal of cursing and puffing, the sheriff laid out the dead man in the cell next to Mel. 'Old goat,' he muttered. 'About as likely a cattle thief as Mary's boy child.'

Mel silently watched the sheriff from under the brim of his hat. He was truly in two minds about a man dying or getting himself killed. The Cree in him believed there was a greater place to go to; the white man thought it was simply turning your toes to the daisies.

He pulled his hat over his face, clasped his fingers behind his head, and closed his eyes, recalling the time when he'd first realized his own father was getting old.

Hammond Cody had taken him to an eerie, silent place that was the burial ground of Morning Sky. His father had explained how a hand-woven casket containing the body of Mel's mother had been lowered into a shallow grave. There had been ritual songs, and for her final journey she was buried with a pair of moccasins and a few personal belongings. Mel had watched intrigued as his pa kneeled to place one of two bone effigies into the bower of branches. At the time, there was so much Mel had wanted to ask about medicine and spiritual meanings, but he was embarrassed and unsure, because he was a child. That was when he'd noticed the wolfy greyness of his pa's hair, the deeply etched lines of his aging.

The pieces of moose bone had been carved into small animals, and Mel still kept one of them deep in his pocket. Now, lying in his close darkness, he envisioned a cunning smirk across Budge Miner's face and shuddered. He shook himself from his daydream and pulled his hat away from his face. For a moment he reflected on allowing himself to be drawn into trouble. He'd only been in Polvo Gris an hour or so, but he swore that before he left, he'd have a go at shifting that look off Miner's face.

3

Except for childbirth, tooth-pulling and sickly calves, George McLane MD didn't regard anything less than amputations as very serious. 'I can take it off now. But if it's fixing up you're after, come back when the fighting stops,' was a quoted truism from his sawbones days in the Civil War.

He pushed up out of his chair, flustered when the cowhand, Wystan Rourke, piled into his private room in the back of his surgery. Through the door he could see Budge Miner waiting on the back porch with Miles Beckman and Felix Chelloe.

Rourke turned his bloodied arm toward him. 'I been hit. This goddamn arm's fallin' apart. See to it, Doc.'

McLane appraised the man's shattered limb. 'Looks to me like someone's already done just that.'

'Just get on with it,' Rourke yelled. 'Stop the pain an' the bleeding.'

'We'll use the surgery,' McLane said. He walked into the annexed room and rinsed his hands then slowly reached for a towel.

Rourke followed him, standing close by and cursing under his breath. He was blanched with pain, his face greasy-cold with sweat. 'Goddamn you, McLane. You waiting for the gangrene?'

'That's what you'll get if I don't clean my hands,' McLane said calmly. 'There's plenty worse off than you today. Are you the one who killed Selwyn?'

'You know about that?'

'I knew he'd been shot dead . . . not who pulled the trigger.'

Rourke took short, sharp breaths and glared at the doctor. 'He drew on me. I just defended myself.'

McLane took hold of the cuff of Rourke's shirt. He lifted it up for a closer look at the bullet wound between the man's wrist and elbow. Rourke let out a gasp of pain and staggered back a step.

'What the hell you doing, you idiot? The goddamn arm's broke! Been smashed with a bullet – anyone can see that. Give me something for the pain before you start meddling.'

'You best remember, sonny, this meddling idiot's the only one around here who can do something for you.' The doctor was upset and his smile showed it. 'Anyway, a top ranny who's tough enough to take out Selwyn Church in a gun fight can endure a twinge or two. But if you want that help, it'll cost you ten dollars.'

'Ten dollars?'

'Yep. The bones're busted, and need some fancy work. It's ten dollars, and I hope you're carrying it in your left pocket. Take it or leave it, mister; it ain't my body.'

Rourke gasped. 'Why you bloodsucker. I'll—' But the man stopped short of his threat when Budge Miner strode into the surgery.

'I can hear you squealing on the street,' he complained. 'Sounds like a pig with a stick up its ass.'

'He wants ten dollars for fixin' my arm,' Rourke rasped. 'He ain't a doctor, he's an old army cutthroat.'

'And I want it before I start,' McLane said coolly, his manner matching Miner's.

Miner turned on Rourke. 'Wash the wound yourself. We'll just take some painkilling stuff. Waste of time coming to this dude set-up. We should've gone to the livery for a saddle-stitch. He'd've charged five dollars for a lasting job.'

McLane almost smiled. *If only he knew.* 'I just told him. It looks like there's bad lesion trouble . . . all sorts of trauma, besides broken bone,' he said instead.

Miner grabbed the lapels of McLane's coat and shoved him into a high-backed chair.

'You shut your mouth,' he said, and kicked the doctor's shin with the sharp toe of his boot. 'We need something to clean his wound.'

He went to a glass-fronted cabinet and looked at the labels on bottles. He opened the door and pulled out a bottle of laudanum. 'We'll take this. Let's go, Stan,' he said, and tossed a silver dollar onto McLane's desk.

McLane glared defiantly. 'A bully's always a coward, Miner. I've seen 'em all in my time. And there's one thing they all got in common. They die many times, and you ain't no different. Your time's coming. It's just a question of how far away.'

Miner's jaw tightened. He hesitated, then left, shoving Rourke ahead of him.

Miner clumped down the steps of McLane's property and shouted at Felix Chelloe. 'Get back to Mr Spool. Tell him what's happened. We'll sort out the drifter. We'll bring the supply wagon in early tomorrow. Have the boys make a gather on the cattle.'

Chelloe went off at a canter. Miner led Rourke and Miles Beckman down the street to Marcella's Quarter.

'We'll wait here an hour,' he said. 'Then, Miles, you go and bail out the 'breed.'

Beckman grimaced, 'Bail out the 'breed? I don't understand. Why are we bailing *him* out?'

'Because he's no good to us in Vaughn's jail.' Miner beckoned the bartender and ordered beer. 'You'll get your chance, Miles. We'll bust him up some when he gets out. Then we'll get him back on that grey of his.' Miner could see both Beckman and Rourke eying him intently, still not completely understanding. 'We ain't got Church any more, remember? So we need someone else. Like the 'breed.'

Beckman's mouth opened as he grasped Miner's plan. 'We got ourselves a pigeon to take the blame. We pull the big job, and he's there, prime an' sassy,' he said, tapping the side of his nose and grinning foxily.

Beer was placed on the bar in front of the three men who stood indifferent to the stares of the other customers. Not one of them doubted that the ill feeling in Polvo Gris was already running high against them. That had started from the time Casper Spool cut himself off from the range and the town to become his own law.

'*You* drink some of this,' Miner said, pulling out the bottle of laudanum that he'd taken from Doc McLane's surgery. 'When we get you back to the ranch, we'll get that arm seen to proper,' he told Rourke with little obvious feeling.

Doc McLane limped across the hot sandy street. He grimaced, his face tilted away from the low glare of the sun. His leg hurt from where Miner had kicked him.

Selwyn Church had been a friend, and it was crazy for anyone to believe he'd been involved in something to get shot for.

25

He stepped through the open door of the jail-house to find Sheriff Vaughn seated behind his desk, an unlit corn-cob pipe in the corner of his mouth. The sheriff raised his eyes wearily. He held a dipping pen and had been concentrating on writing up a ledger.

'You took your time,' he grumbled. 'But before you say anything, George, there was nothing I could do about Rourke killing old Selwyn. It was done when I got there.'

'Yeah, well, I guess our legs just don't carry their full, fast movement any more, Brett,' McLane answered sardonically. He looked through to the cells at Mel. He'd seen Mel ride in, and been interested. Lone riders were rare in Polvo Gris and a stranger who'd travelled so long and so far to get here was an added curiosity.

'You're not really a cattle rustler are you, son?' he asked directly.

Mel lay still on the cot. Only his eyes moved as he took in the other man. 'No, I ain't. Sheriff thinks otherwise though, an' that's what counts from in here.'

'Ha,' McLane laughed. 'Even *I* know that Indians are only *horse thieves*.' He turned to confront the sheriff.

Vaughn got in first. 'I can do without the smart remarks, George.'

'You're a damn fool, Brett, and most of this town knows it. A good sheriff? Yes. A damn fool, nonetheless.

You really believe what them Spool hands are saying? They treat this town as if it's their own private robbers' roost. They're goddamn irritants at best, and never been far away from a killing at worst, and that's now. So close your chops and listen to me for a bit,' McLane advised. 'I was out front having myself a smoke when I saw old Selwyn ride into town. He came in past the chandlers . . . the other end of town. That's what he would have done if he'd been coming from his ranch. But I saw this stranger too, and there was a good half-hour between them. He comes in from the north though, where he would have if he'd come off the Colorado trail.'

The sheriff quietly contemplated his desk top, rubbing his chin and inspecting the bowl of his pipe.

'Come on, Brett,' McLane persisted. 'You already heard him say he's no rustler. I believe him, why can't you? In fact, why don't you release him, let him get about his business? The only harm he's likely to do now will be to Spool's crew.'

Mel rolled from his cot. He stepped up to the bars of his cell and looked intensely at Doc McLane. 'I'm obliged for that.'

McLane held out his hand. 'Name's George McLane. For my sins, town MD.'

'I'm Mel Cody.' He pushed his own hand through the bars to shake hands. 'Just tell me why.'

'Always prided myself on having the measure of a man,' McLane replied. 'Sheriff knows it, too. He also

27

knows I don't condone wasting town's money. That's what'll happen if there's a court case over this.'

Vaughn dabbed at the sweaty sheen across his face. 'Miner said he followed two sets of tracks into town from Selwyn's place. He said Cody here was in league with him.'

'Budge Miner's about as wholesome as Injun whiskey, and we all know it.' McLane turned casually to Mel. 'Sorry, son, no offence meant.'

'None taken.'

'If you want, I'll document those facts,' McLane told Vaughn. 'Whichever way it breaks, young Mel here doesn't deserve to be locked up for going to old Selwyn's aid. If it was you or me, Brett, we'd have done the same thing. Sure we'd be dead, but that's the only difference.'

Undecided as to what action to take, Vaughn lifted his hands from Mel's gun, and gripped the edges of his desk. Aware of the lawman's dilemma, McLane stepped forward and pulled a ring of keys from a wall peg. But Vaughn grunted and clasped a big hand around the man's wrist.

'Goddamnit, Doc. I'm sitting here willing to listen to you, not have you take over the jail.'

McLane sighed wearily, and dropped the keys onto the end of the desk. 'I was only wanting you to move. We've said all there is.'

'There's more, Doc, an' you know it. I got to put this side of things to Miner. Then, depending on what he says and what we work out, I'll either release Cody or keep him here for trial.' Vaughn smiled patiently at McLane. 'As a doctor, George, you'd make a decent bulldogger. Now leave me alone to get on with my work.'

McLane grimaced exasperatedly as Vaughn hung the keys back on the wall hook. Then he turned to give Mel a friendly-like wink. 'Tell me what happened, son. I suddenly got myself a bedside manner.'

'I'll go lay down again then,' Mel said wryly.

4

Mel started to explain to Doc McLane. 'I saw Church being crowded . . . figured there was too many for him,' he said. 'I told Miner that, but he wasn't impressed. I had to step in – stop the beating. The old man could only just about stand, but he made a break for it. An' that was the wrong move . . . the curious thing about it.'

'What's so *curious* about what?' McLane asked.

'Well, he could . . . should have gotten clear, but he didn't. He stopped an' pulled a gun, he was so stirred up. I could see it in his eyes. He managed to get off a shot too. That's when Rourke killed him.'

'Selwyn said something? Before he died?' McLane asked.

'He didn't have time to say much. He mumbled something though – something about him not being a cattle stealer.' Mel turned thoughtfully toward McLane. 'I guess you'd expect that. But I just got the feeling it meant more ... don't know why or what. That's about it. The sheriff arrived then. You can ask him what happened next.'

McLane turned to Vaughn for an explanation, but before he had time to ask anything, Miles Beckman stepped into the jailhouse.

The Spool rider chinked some coin in his hand, placed it down carefully on Vaughn's desk. 'Budge's been doing some figuring ... reckons he could be wrong, Sheriff,' he said.

'That'll be a first,' McLane answered back.

'Yeah, well as there's a doubt, he figures you won't be talking bail,' Beckman replied. 'So here's ten dollars for the inconvenience.' Then he ran his eyes over Mel and, with the trace of a smirk, made for the open doorway.

As he was about to step onto the boardwalk, Vaughn yelled, 'Not so fast, cowboy.'

Beckman looked back insolently. 'If ten ain't enough ... too bad. Take it up with Budge. I done my bit.'

Vaughn took a couple of steps toward the cowhand. 'What about the charges he made?' he snapped. 'We just forget, do we?'

Beckman shrugged. 'Like I said. He reckons he could've been wrong. That's it.' And with that, Beckman was gone.

While Vaughn was staring nonplussed out into the street, Mel removed his sash, smiled wryly and offered a key-turning motion in response.

Doc McLane picked up the cell keys, called Vaughn's name and tossed them to him. 'You got no reason to hold him, Brett,' he said. 'At least you made ten dollars out of his board.'

Vaughn caught the keys. He fidgeted with them a few moments, then unlocked Mel's cell. 'No hard feelings, son,' he said. 'I was just doing my job.'

Mel picked up his hat and tugged it back on his head. He collected his gun from the desk, checked the cylinder and quickly pushed it into his coat pocket. 'I know it.'

'There is one thing I'd like to know,' the sheriff asked.

'What's that, Sheriff?'

'What do you intend to do now?'

'First off, I'm going to see my horse is OK. Then I'm going to get me some rib sticker an' wash it down with a bottle of whiskey. That'll be white man's, of course,' he added with a quick ironic look at McLane. 'I need to wash the taste of this hog-pen out of my mouth. After that I don't know. I really don't.'

'Yeah, well that's the part I'm interested in. I suggest you keep riding,' Vaughn said. 'Miner ain't fooling me with that *could be wrong* stuff. An' I don't want you tangling with him.'

'I don't want me tangling with him either. But that's up to him,' Mel said, and followed Beckman out onto the street.

Vaughn took a step forward, but McLane dropped a restraining hand on his arm. 'Easy there, Brett. You've done your best by that boy. Now leave well enough alone.'

'If he goes down to Marcella's an' Miner's there with the others, they'll bust him. Hell, you know that.'

'Yeah, I know it. At least I know they'll try.' McLane's eyes gleamed with the prospect.

Vaughn noticed and rumbled an oath. 'Damn you, George. You had that in mind when you first came over. You spoke up for that 'breed drifter just to get him back out there . . . back on the street.'

'Time Miner was pegged down, Brett. I haven't seen anyone much in the last few months who could do it . . . not until now. You want to move some checkers . . . fill in the time?'

'Did you see what young Cody did with that fancy binding he was wearing round his middle?'

'Yeah, he wound it up real neat-like an' put it in his pocket.'

'What for? Why'd he do that?'

'Dunno. Perhaps he doesn't want to get it messed up. Why don't you go and ask him? You know where he's headed.'

'Yeah I just might, by Christ. If them rough-stringers start cutting up again, I'll send 'em back to

Spool short-handed. An' Cody along with 'em, if he answers their call.' The lawman stomped to his desk. He buckled his gunbelt back on and pushed his pipe into a top pocket, his mouth chewing over a fitting threat. He slammed his desk drawer closed, tossed the ring of cell keys at the wall peg, and cursed when they missed, clattering on the floor.

Doc McLane went out onto the boardwalk and squinted into the falling sun. A moment later he called back to Vaughn. 'No need to hurry, Brett. Our boy's going where he said. He's looking out for that grey of his.'

Vaughn pushed some papers into a heap on his desk. With a purposeful tug at the brim of his old Stetson he joined McLane on the boardwalk.

The doctor pointed to the land west of town where a trail ran in a thin line across the plain. It was late afternoon but heat still shimmered across the land. Dust was rising to make a low cloud between Polvo Gris and Buckskin Mountain's timbered slopes. 'The stage's coming in. Be here in ten, fifteen minutes,' he said. Then he laughed and started off across the street. 'Should give you something else to worry about,' he called out over his shoulder.

After Mel gave Bill Frater's boy instructions on how to tend his horse, he went out to the street. He stood a moment, listening to the low rolling rumble of wheels and the creak of harness above the day's afternoon stillness. He saw a coach bumping its way across the hard country, heard the driver yipping at the team in his final dash for town.

Townsfolk emerged from stores to stand expectantly along the boardwalks. There was no practical reason for them to meet the stage. They simply needed to see, to get touched by events and happenings distant from their own isolated frontier town.

Mel turned on his heel and walked toward the saloon. He allowed himself a moment's thought for Budge Miner and the sheriff's warning about retaliation. But he was too thankful to be away from his confinement to give time to Miner and his colleagues.

He was close to Marcella's Quarter when, ahead and to his right, a rider emerged from an alleyway. Mel recognized him as one of Miner's company – Beckman, one of the two who'd stood back while Selwyn Church was killed. But the man paid Mel no heed, turning out of the narrow lane and moving on along the street.

Mel stopped walking and took a step back beneath an overhang. Only when Beckman went on by did he step out again.

The noise of the stage was close, swelling in the street around him. Mel found a place with a good view and watched. His eyes glittered with anticipation as the racing coach horses raced round the final turn into town.

The break from his inborn watchfulness made Mel unprepared for the big loop of rope that suddenly dropped over his shoulders. For the briefest moment he was confused, then his hands jerked up, taking hold of the tightening rope as he heeled about. The drag by the rider in the street wrenched Mel from the boardwalk, but he caught sight of two more men as they rode from the alley. He was pulled off balance, falling when he recognized the leering face of Budge Miner. For the shortest moment he thought of rescue when Brett Vaughn yelled out from somewhere behind him.

He twisted his body as he landed, but the side of his face still slammed into the hard-packed surface of the street. He sucked in a mouthful of alkali dust, spat and grabbed up along the taut line of the rope. Miles Beckman brazenly wheeled his horse and kicked it into a lunging run.

Mel was dragged on his chest for several yards before a hard-baked runnel turned him over. He went with the movement, getting onto his back. After another twenty or thirty more yards, he drew up his legs, and dug his heels in. It was the sort of punishment he knew about, and could deal with. He'd heard other tales from his grandfather, Chief Josef Fish, learned how braves had tested themselves for strength and vision. But right now, and like a lot of things Indian, Mel only had the legend to go by.

With Beckman now whooping with excitement,

Mel twisted over onto his chest again, making a desperate clutch up the rope's length to gain a grip higher up. He swung his legs around into an arc, pressing his knees into the ground and giving one tremendous jerk. Momentarily the rope slackened and, half-bent, he lumbered to his feet, staggering a few steps. He leaned back against the rope, and braced his legs. Then he hauled with all his angered strength. He looked up and, from the middle of the street, saw the stagecoach bearing down on him. Having thrown caution to the wind, Miner and another man were riding along the trail of his dust.

Sheriff Vaughn yelled, wildly, as he ran forward, and from the edge of his porch, Doc McLane swore freely. The town's dog pack crouched in a semi-circle beneath the boardwalk. Their hackles were raised and they barked madly at the noise and disorder.

Mel saw everything fleetingly before he saw the alarmed eyes of the coach driver. The driver dragged frantically on the reins with one hand, the brake lever with the other. Beckman, meanwhile, to control his kicking, frightened mount, had eased off the rope and Mel dragged him from his saddle. As the coach veered around him, Mel moved forward. He pulled the slack rope from his upper body, closing in on the man who was scrambling to his knees.

Mel wasted no time. With both hands he grabbed Beckman's lank hair, and dragged him up. 'That's a bad thing you just done. What have I ever done to you?' he rasped, staring into the man's craven eyes.

He hit the man in the stomach with his left hand, pushing his head back down with his right. He brought up his knee sharply, groaning in mutual torment as he sensed Beckman's teeth snapping through his tongue. Then he stepped back. The man stared at his boots as the blood dripped, making thick globules in the dirt between them.

Mel chopped swiftly at Beckman's neck with the side of his hand, watching impassively as he went down. '*Now*, you got an answer.'

5

Mel turned to see the stage had slowed around him. He'd felt the air pulse as the big, iron-bound hubs of the wheels churned within inches of his lower back. The heavy vehicle had gone on another twenty yards, had torn out the boardwalk railings of Polvo Gris's boarding-house before coming to rest with its near-side door only a few feet off the depot's landing stage. The driver, huffing and puffing, turned to look back at Mel as he approached. Two young ranch hands ran to control the frightened horses, hanging onto lead traces while the driver swung himself down from his box. The rear off-side window blind unfurled and the face of a young woman looked out. She glanced quickly at Mel and the agitated crowd and pushed the knuckles of her fist against her chin. He had time to see the foreboding in her bright eyes.

Then the pounding of hoofs bore down on him. He went into a crouch, turning in time to see Budge

Miner swing himself from his horse. With one hand the big man was gripping his saddle-horn ready to launch himself.

Mel braced his legs and raised his hands. As Miner crashed down on him, he grabbed at the man's leather coat. He swung the ox of a man around then let go. He darted back a yard before Miner's shoulder hit the ground. But the man was agile: he rolled with the impact and came up cursing to face Mel.

Mel braced himself as Miner came at him. The man was wild. He wanted a fight and lashed out with a flurry of blows. One smashed into the side of Mel's head and he went back on his heels. He dodged aside as Miner continued to swing at him.

Mel caught two more glancing blows before he regained his balance. He dipped under a wild swing and brought his clenched knuckles up under Miner's jaw. The heavy man was jolted, but he'd been ready. He set his thick neck, tucked his head in and bunched his shoulder muscles. He took the blow well – that blow and another that Mel shafted in at his meaty face. There was a flat splatter of noise, a split second's respite before Miner opened up, breaking into Mel's attack with machine-like ferocity.

Mel backed off, his senses working. As Miner pursued him, the two men fought their way across the street. A crowd milled around them, keeping wide in an expanding circle. Sheriff Vaughn yelled again, but this time it was close. Then he saw McLane pacing alongside the fight.

Mel thought he'd got the measure of his opponent. He could take a breath, pick his spot and consider the blow. He almost grinned as he ducked a great looping right. He stopped, then dashed forward and drove a straight right to Miner's forehead. As the man's head shook, Mel sent in another with the same hand. Pain stabbed through the bones of his fingers and wrist as he connected with teeth. Miner was done, but he lumbered on. His eyes glazed and spitting blood, he made low guttural noises from his smashed mouth.

'Goddamn you two. Cut it out,' Vaughn shouted.

Mel heard the sheriff above the clamour of the excited crowd. But he didn't need to act on it – and Miner wasn't going to pay Vaughn any heed.

Mel breathed deep, bit his lip at the pain along his hand and forearm. He turned to have a look at the stagecoach. The girl was still looking from the window. Her eyes met his and he could see the troubled look in her colour-drained face.

The stage driver was telling her something, but the girl's attention had been seized by what she was witnessing in the street.

Budge Miner had found the life to come back at Mel, and he was close. He roared in with both hands around Mel's neck, and bent him backwards. Mel brought up the heel of his boot, catching Miner full and hard. He felt the man's tough fingers loosen and

41

he spun himself around fast. He was up close to the man's bloodied face and he didn't like it. He remembered his pa once telling him the big ones went down hardest. It just took them a bit longer.

Mel wrenched himself free, at the same time jabbing his left hand hard all over Miner's face, then his neck. Each time Miner's head came straight, he hit him again with a blow to the opposite side of his head. Hard against bone, the flesh of Miner's cheek split open and blood gushed, then an eyebrow was torn.

Both Mel's arms were hurting and he took a small step back to finish Miner off. He half-turned away and swung up his foot to catch Miner hard around his back, deep in his kidneys – a blow that a one-time Blackfoot friend had taught him many years before. This was the end for Miner and Mel knew it. He watched with satisfaction as the big man staggered around in a tight circle.

Miner caught sight of the coach and reached out for it. He got his hands on the windowsill and looked up into the terrified face of the girl. She gasped and shrunk away. Miner laughed before his legs gave in and he crumpled heavily to the street.

Mel wiped the blood from the torn skin of his knuckles. His ribs and most of his body hurt, and he breathed in short shallow gasps. But his head cleared and he rubbed at his mouth with his coat sleeve.

The crowd had gone silent now. Most of the people were silently watching Mel. It was the first time they'd seen the like done to Budge Miner.

Vaughn angrily pushed two onlookers aside, as he stepped down from the boardwalk. In the yellow light of the late afternoon sun, he walked slowly toward the coach. 'Okay, Cody,' he growled. 'We both know he had it coming. Now move away.'

Mel looked tiredly at the lawman but said nothing. He looked to the window of the coach and his heart pounded. The girl was staring directly at him. Her lips moved and she shook her head.

Doc McLane called out anxiously. 'Look out!' The sheriff and Mel swung around.

Wystan Rourke came reeling along the boardwalk. He was beyond the coach team, dragging a leg, his right arm hanging useless at his side. In his out-stretched left he gripped a long-barrelled Colt. He swung the barrel at Mel.

'Damn your hide, Rourke! Put the gun down,' Vaughn yelled.

But Wystan Rourke had come too far to back off. He passed behind the coach and its team, pushed his back up against the wall of the stage-depot building. With his blood racing, he'd sucked recklessly at the laudanum. His eyes were red-rimmed, filled with hopeless loathing. He gasped, managed to hold his breath as he attempted a careful aim.

He bared his teeth and was ready to kill, when Mel

43

went for his own Colt. He pulled the gun and actioned off one shot before Rourke had the chance to fire.

The roar split the pall of silence. A woman shrieked and the dogs opened up again with their barking. As echoes rebounded across the town, Mel's bullet hammered high into Rourke's chest. The man couldn't go back; he just slid down the clapped wall, sat cross-legged and died. His head lolled forward and the last of the day's light slanted sharp across his shirt front, partly hiding the spreading stain.

Mel looked at the coach. The girl was no longer watching from the window. Miner hadn't stirred, but Beckman, the man who'd started the fight with his thrown lariat, was moving forward.

Beckman's vindictive glare drilled into Mel. But the sheriff had been watching him and had seen him rise from the street where Mel had dumped him. He pulled his Colt and levelled it at Beckman.

'Don't, Beckman,' he shouted. 'Just get back.'

Beckman thought for a second, then, dragging his hand across the blood that ran from his chin, he lowered his gun.

Mel stepped away from Vaughn's side. 'They ain't ever going to give in, are they, Sheriff?'

Vaughn swore to himself. 'Like hell they won't. This fight's over,' he stated for the attention of every-one. 'The next man, woman or child who goes for a gun will find themselves half-full of buckshot an' laid out on George's bench, God help me.' He walked toward Rourke and pushed at the body with his boot. 'He must have wanted this real bad,' he muttered before turning back to Beckman.

'You get Miner on his horse . . . get him out of my sight . . . out of this town. Tell Spool what happened here, an' make sure you tell him as it was. He can deal with any of Rourke's kin . . . not that any will own up to it. That goes for both o' you. Now get out.'

Beckman grumbled as he turned his attention to Miner. He dragged at the big man's clothing. As a dead weight, though, Miner was too much for him.

'Go get their horses,' Vaughn ordered one of the youngsters who'd been holding onto the coach team's harness.

A few minutes later, he asked both boys to get Miner across the saddle of his horse. 'The town'll take care of Rourke,' he told Beckman when the man had painfully mounted his own horse. Beckman looked bitterly at Mel. He opened his mouth to spit out the last say when Vaughn snarled, 'Remember, you're through here, Beckman. Now get out an' stay out. Ride.'

Mel stood, undaunted and unmoved. He took his waistband from his pocket and thoughtfully looped it around his middle. Beckman watched as he turned his horse down the street and walked on, Miner's horse trailing nervously behind.

Vaughn watched silently until Beckman rode to

the end of the main street, then turned to Mel. 'Well, what now? You finished the show or what? Perhaps another act to close with?'

'No, I ain't got any more. You saw what happened,' Mel told him straight.

'Yeah, I saw. The whole goddamn town saw . . . got impressed too. But I'm thinking you and Polvo Gris ain't ideally suited. Might be for the best if you rode on as well.'

Mel didn't answer. He looked away toward Eagle Tail Mountains. He thought maybe he *should* ride on, see if he could find which particular part of the country his pa meant him to make *his*.

Vaughn stepped past him and had another look at Rourke. He asked the two boys to carry the dead cowhand to Bill Frater's livery stable, then he started to get the street cleared, dispersing the crowd. He looked at the driver then to the girl. 'To some of us this is all in a day's work. I guess you can carry on with your business.'

The doc stood outside Scullys. He was smoking one of his cigaritos and holding a glass of whiskey. Vaughn, passing close by, noticed the doctor's satisfaction.

'There ain't going to be any more trouble out here, George,' he growled. 'Why don't you get off the street, too?'

'All I've been doing is putting forward my opinion.

46

The fact that it's evidence isn't exactly my fault, or what ensued,' he railed in good humour.

'You interfering old duffer. Don't try an' soft-soap me,' Vaughn retorted. 'We both know who was ring-leading all this.'

McLane shook his head and grinned mischie-vously as the sheriff started back along the street toward his jailhouse.

The stagecoach team was now standing quiet. After tying off the reins, and setting the handbrake, the driver went to the side door and opened it, almost immediately calling out for the doc.

McLane put down his glass, threw his smoke aside and hurriedly crossed the street. The moment he saw the girl's stockinged legs, he shoved the driver out of the way, and climbed into the coach. He could see the girl was pale, but she appeared unhurt.

'Sitting in here's not ideal for anyone's constitu-tion,' he called out to Vaughn who'd returned to the coach on hearing the driver shout.

'Who is she?' Vaughn asked of the driver.

'Came from Yuma. Name's R. Church,' said the driver who was craning his neck for a look.

'Church?' Vaughn asked.

'R. Church. That's what it says on the passenger list, an' on the luggage tags,' the driver answered. 'You want that I should help, Doc?'

'No,' McLane said simply. 'Just move her luggage to the depot. I can send somebody for it later.'

The doc eased the girl to her feet and into Vaughn's arms, then climbed down. 'We'll take her to my place, poor kid. What a first sight this must have been for her. No wonder she headed for the floor.'

As she came to, the two men helped her across the street, down to the end of town. They made her comfortable on a couch in McLane's front room, then after McLane lifted a window full open, they went out onto the porch.

'You hear that name, George?' Vaughn asked.

'Yeah. You don't reckon. . . ?' he said, the question tailing off.

'Don't know. I got other things to take care of.' Vaughn cast a jaundiced eye up and down the now quiet street. He lifted a hand in acknowledgement, and made off to administer the burying of Wystan Rourke.

Doctor George McLane was left muttering the girl's name to himself. 'Church,' he said. 'Church. She's got his eyes. It's just got to be . . . goddamnit.'

6

'Well, hello there. You feeling better, young lady?'

In response to the voice, Reba Church raised herself from the couch. For a moment she considered the quiet and unfamiliar surroundings before easing herself back down again. 'Who are you?' she asked, tiredly.

'I'm Willow Legge, and you're not coming to any harm by staying right there, for a while longer, young lady. Your bags are outside in the hallway an' Doctor McLane's in the next room. This is his house.'

The girl wanted her bearings and looked around her uneasily. But Willow's warm smile relaxed her a little.

'What happened?' she asked. 'Where am I?'

'Nothing very much, except you passed out. I'll go fetch the doc, but don't you go bothering to get up now.'

Willow left and a minute or so later, a man came

in. He smiled warmly, took her wrist, and checked her pulse rate.

'As I thought,' he said. 'You're going to live. I'm George McLane, but you can call me Doc. I'm guessing it was the heat inside that coach that made you pass out.'

'I think it was a bit more than that,' the girl said, taking her hand back from McLane's.

'Hmm, I guess you're talking about Budge Miner up close. Huh, he's no picture even from across the street. It was regrettable that you had to get such a ringside view. Miss Church, isn't it?'

'Yes. Rebecca Church,' the girl said. 'But you can call me Reba,' she added, with a glint in her eye. 'I'm looking for my uncle Selwyn Church.'

McLane turned slightly away and swallowed hard.

'Is there something wrong?' Reba asked. 'Dr McLane?'

When McLane finally turned back, his face was drawn. His eyes looked heavy under his grey brows. 'Yes, I'm afraid there is,' he said. 'Your uncle's dead, Rebecca . . . Reba. He was killed today . . . just today here in town. There was another fight. I'm real sorry.'

Reba shook her head. 'Another fight?'

'Yes. What you saw was the aftermath of it, I guess. The one who's dead in the street? Well . . . he's the one . . . that . . .'

'. . . killed my uncle,' Reba said, finishing the doc's

sentence for him.

McLane nodded. 'I am very sorry. Selwyn was a friend as well as a patient. Not close, but a friend nevertheless. He was a good man. There's more than a few people in this town who did know him well, and they'll miss him. Not one of them could've stopped what happened, though.'

'Why not? What did happen?'

'He got involved in an argument with some cowhands from out of town, and went for his gun. He was killed for it.'

'You said *them*. How many did it take?' Reba asked, the hurt and frailty obvious in her voice.

'It was just the one,' McLane said quietly.

Reba blinked, but it was more shocked than tearful. 'I wanted to tell him . . . ask him if I could help. There was nothing left for me up north.' There was a short silence, then she added, 'I knew I wasn't headed for the promised land but. . . .' She shook her head and let the words trail away.

McLane felt her silent anguish. He was unable to come up with words that made sense of her arrival in town, the timing. 'Well you're safe here,' he said, and quietly left the room. He asked Willow to look after her, to engage her in small talk, said he wanted to keep her in the house for a while. 'I'm thinking this place was more peaceable when we arrived,' he muttered drily.

At Marcella's he ordered a beer and whiskey chaser. Mel Cody was standing at the end of the counter with Brett Vaughn, and he got a round for them too. He held the beer in his right hand and pushed the whiskeys along the counter with his left. 'The girl's Selwyn's niece. I think she'll be staying for a while,' he said, to ease their curiosity.

'His niece, eh? I did wonder on it. She's come a long way to find him dead,' the sheriff replied.

'Yeah, ain't that just the hell of it?' McLane agreed in a raw manner. 'She can't be more than twenty, and all I can do is take her pulse and tell her what a lot of friends Selwyn had in town. What sort of prattle-gob does that make me, eh?'

Mel had been studying the doctor's face. 'Are you talking about the girl in the stage?'

'The very one. I reckon she saw most of the fight, if not all of it. That's why she blacked out . . . the horror of it all. And who's to blame her? She's likely never seen anything quite like the street show you put on out there.'

Vaughn looked up from his whiskey and nodded. 'Yeah, it's a cheerless story sure enough, but that's about all it is, eh, Doc? I don't see what we can do about it. Besides, I've got other stuff to take care of.'

The doc gave him the beady eye. 'Oh, yeah. You've got paperwork for a burial to take care of. Very tiresome.'

'No, I've taken care of that. I'm talking about

young Mel here.'

'I don't need taking care of,' Mel told him with good humour.

The sheriff flicked a shrewd eye at the doctor. 'Oh, yes you do, son. Oh, yes you do. Tell him, George. Tell him what Miner'll do when he gets his senses back.'

'He'll rant some, make threats and get his drawers twisted,' McLane mumbled casually.

'He'll buckle on his gunbelt, that's what he'll do, goddamnit! He's soaked up a punishment here in town today. That's humiliation for Miner. He ramrods the biggest spread in the territory and keeps the hands in check 'cause they're scared of him . . . scared to hell. As sure as the sun comes up tomorrow he'll be back to save his face.' The sheriff turned to Mel and poked him in the chest. 'He'll come to town looking for you, an' it won't be to shoot the breeze. So you just sup that whiskey an' get that nice-looking grey saddled. You hear me?'

'I hear you, Sheriff,' Mel told him.

Doc McLane looked on curiously. 'Where are you headed for?'

'I don't remember saying I was headed anywhere,' Mel said, again with the good-humoured smile.

Vaughn cracked the base of his glass against the counter. 'Maybe you was too good for Rourke, son. But Miner with a gun's another proposition. I told you, he won't be looking to do you any favours. He's cunning. We'll never know he's there, 'til it's too late. You'll never know. I don't want any more trouble in town. Not while I'm still sheriff.'

'There's half of me that makes it difficult for a man like Miner to gain much of an advantage, Sheriff,' Mel said drily.

'I bet I know which half,' the doc added.

'A man shouldn't have to ride from anywhere for no reason,' Mel continued.

Vaughn was getting exasperated. 'You got a reason. I'm *telling* you . . . ain't asking.'

Doc McLane saw the expression that set Mel's face and hardened his eyes. He was reminded again of the first time he'd seen the man ride into town. Since then, Mel Cody had bested Budge Miner and three of his cowboy cronies in a side street. Later, set upon by three of them, he'd got out of Beckman's roping, given Miner another beating and shot Wystan Rourke dead. McLane knew his instincts were right about Melvin Cody. The Indian part troubled him, the part that had re-tied the beaded sash, the fearless part.

'I rode hundreds of miles to reach Polvo Gris, Sheriff,' Mel said. 'It's my pa's homeland, an' he wanted me to see it. So far I can't see the attraction, but I promised him I'd have a look. You ain't going to change that. I haven't done anything wrong.'

'Listen to me, son. Maybe you're right, maybe you ain't done nothing wrong. But all you're going to do is cause trouble by staying around. Let's face it, you ain't even got yourself a pot to piss in. Your only board was my jail. So, as it is. . . .'

'As it is, you best clear the decks, Brett,' McLane interjected. 'The boy's not so much a drifter as you might think.'

'Stay out of this, George. You've been dancing with enough trouble today already.'

'Can't do that, Brett. Wouldn't be fair on Mel.'

'What the hell's fair got to do with it?' the sheriff demanded, looking quizzically at Mel.

'He's got himself work,' McLane continued. 'The Church girl needs help out at Selwyn's place. At least 'til probate's done. I suggested she take on Mel.'

Vaughn's jaw dropped. He indicated for the bartender to pour them another round of whiskeys. 'You joshing me?'

McLane ran some coin onto the counter for the whiskey. 'No, I'm serious. I came looking for him. Him and Miss Church have got things to discuss. You don't think I came in here for your company do you, you old woosher?'

'You probably thought, "here's where the next load of trouble's coming from",' Vaughn grumbled.

The doctor studied his whiskey. 'Seems to me you could be a tad more appreciative, Brett. Maybe get the town to award him one of them civic-duty badges. Rourke's not going to be missed, and Cody handed Miner nothing more than he's been asking for for a long time. You tell me what's so wrong with that? Look at it from the girl's point of view. She gets here to find herself in the middle of a gunfight, then finds out her uncle's been shot dead. She's no one to turn to. Putting young Mel to work's not such a dumb idea. Have you got a problem with that, eh Brett?'

'Selwyn's land rests smack-bang up against the Spool spread. In case you forgot, Budge Miner ramrods it. Have I got any problems with that? You out of your mind?'

Doc McLane grinned. 'Yeah. Isn't that good?' he said, with a roguish twinkle in his eye.

'By hell, I could probably get you for disturbing the peace or something similar . . . toss you in a cell even, for that,' Vaughn retorted.

'Wouldn't do any good, Brett. Least of all Cosmo Collins and his waterbelly trouble. The Fulpott woman's expecting to drop another child any day, and then there's Ma—'

'Gaaargh.' Vaughn picked up his drink and finished it in one gulp. 'To hell with everybody. Don't know why I bother to even try an' keep the peace in this hell-hole.'

He glowered at Mel, then back to McLane.

'I'll be glad when they call time on this day.' The sheriff coughed, wiped his chin and walked dourly from the saloon.

McLane raised his eyebrows and took a sip of the remainder of his drink. 'I know what you're thinking,

56

son. I'm ready when you are.'

Mel finished his drink. 'Is that the truth . . . what you just told the sheriff?'

McLane grinned. 'The idea of it was. I got the notion you want to stick around, Sheriff Vaughn or Budge Miner notwithstanding.'

Mel raised his chin, studied the doctor.

'If that means what I think it means, I need some more time here . . . roundabouts.'

'Are you looking for something particular?' McLane asked.

'Don't rightly know. Did you know that girl . . . before today?'

'Rebecca Church? Never seen her before. I'm not so sure Old Selwyn had either. I guess he would have said something if he had.' McLane was thoughtful for a few seconds, then said, 'I got myself involved now, so I'm kind of obliged to help. If what those Spool men—'

'Hey. Hold up a second, Doc,' Mel interrupted him. 'You're roping me in. You got something else on your mind other than me being some sort of gopher for a white girl? A hay-shaker?'

'Maybe, son. Maybe,' McLane said, smiling uneasily at Mel's belittling turn of phrase. 'If there's trouble there, I'm sure you'll handle it.'

Mel gave a twisted grin and shook his head. 'Then it's no deal. I can find enough of that by just minding my own business.'

'You're in too deep for the luxury of getting by on that, son. Especially in this town. Besides, I've seen enough to know that running scared doesn't figure much in your life. So why not help out the Church girl while you're waiting up? Miner's going to come for you anyway.'

Mel knew that some of what the doc said was true. He stared thoughtfully at the labels on the bottles of drink on the back bar. 'I don't know quite why I came here,' he said, 'but I know it weren't for this.'

McLane leaned across the counter, stood very close. 'Hell, son, if you want to look the ground over, what have you got to lose? No one else is going to employ you. They're too goddamn scared.'

Mel wiped a hand tiredly across his face. 'She sure had a nice face. Her eyes were the same colour as her uncle's. I noticed that.'

'Yeah, that's right, and Selwyn was a good ol' stick by all accounts. He wouldn't have stole a hair from the back of one of those mad dogs out front. From what you say, he was killed saying something to that effect. It wasn't your fault things got out of hand with him getting shot dead, was it? You went to help him.'

'Yeah, that's right,' Mel said falteringly. He wondered if in some curious way, the doc was implicating him, putting some guilt his way.

'And you can't just walk away now, can you, as if nothing's happened?' McLane affirmed. 'There's too much molasses sticking to your legs for that, son.'

Mel gave a few Red River trapper curses. Very soon he would have to consider his next move. Most of his anguish would be caused by those who wanted to get close, side with the town's new champion. But he was a man unused to the press of a crowd, the brush of sudden notoriety.

'Let's go see Miss Church, then,' he said. 'I guess I owe her, 'specially if I'm to blame for the horror of what she's seen and heard so far,' he added ironically.

'That's just fine. Something for us all to look forward to.' McLane beamed and before Mel could change his mind, McLane led the way from the saloon.

7

On entering his house, McLane stopped and looked toward the closed door of his front room. 'How is she?' he asked Willow, who was waiting for him.

'Poorly. I don't think she's taking it well,' Willow replied, her face tight with anxiety. 'I don't think it's my sort of nursing she's after. She's just lying there, staring into space.'

McLane puffed out his cheeks, and fiddled with the cigaritos in his coat pocket. 'Leave it to me, then,' he said. 'Not that it's me or my doctoring she needs either. You better light some more lamps before you get dinner ready, Willow. We'll eat early, eh? Perhaps the smell of home cooking will bring her round. She may well think of leaving after she's more settled and with some food inside her.'

'Oh, I don't think so, Doctor. It's almost full dark now. Where'll she be going in an hour or so?' Willow asked, the concern evident in her voice.

McLane turned to Mel. 'Take a seat, Mel. I won't be a minute,' he said. 'I'll go and see what her thinking is.'

McLane knocked on the door of the room where the girl was resting. There was no response, so he opened the door gently and went in.

Reba Church was sitting up, wedged at the rising end of the couch. She was clasping her hands together, eyes unresponsive as she faced McLane's concern. He could see she'd hardly moved. He took a couple of paces toward her, but she held up a hand that meant she wasn't yet ready.

'I'm sorry,' he said sympathetically. 'In your shoes, I'd probably need more than a couple of hours to recover. I'll leave you for a bit. You know we're here.' McLane backed off, watched her for a moment further, then closed the door quietly.

'I don't think she's too interested in talking about cattle grubs and the like,' he said on rejoining Mel. 'Guess I'll just have to carry on making decisions.'

'And I'll just do the fighting.' Mel had the distinct feeling that McLane had wheedled him into a place he didn't want to be. 'You got the right to make those decisions, Doc?'

'I've got a clear conscience, if that's what you mean. You'll learn that's a good pillow, son . . . lullaby at midnight. You tell me what you or anyone else should do in the circumstances and I'll listen.'

He crossed to a desk in the corner of the room and pulled out paper and a pencil, then sketched a rough map of some country to the north-west of Polvo Gris and handed it to Mel. 'Here, this is your ticket out of trouble. Take a ride, go on out and let some air into the place. Don't know whether Selwyn locked the place up. He didn't have much on him . . . no keys. Have a look around, do anything you figure needs doing. As soon as the girl's well enough to travel, I'll bring her out.'

'An' if I have visitors?' Mel asked.

Doc McLane gave a slight shrug. 'Well if it's not me, it'll be the bad guys, and you fill the place with gunsmoke. Seriously, Mel, I guess you can expect visitors. But you'll get 'em anyway, whether you stay in town or find yourself a hole in a wall somewhere. And remember, this is probably the only way Brett Vaughn's going to let you stick around these parts. Right?'

Mel shrugged. It wasn't quite the answer he was hoping for or expecting. He'd told McLane he wasn't sure what he was looking for in Polvo Gris. That's when he'd lost control of the situation and he knew it – but it was too late now. He picked up his hat. 'How far's this place, then?'

The doc pointed to the map he'd sketched. 'It's a ways. Take you best part of three hours, I reckon. Steer just north of east and keep Standup Rock ahead of you. You'll ford the Dog Creek twice; the second time, head west. Can't miss the place.'

Willow came out and smiled politely. 'Will that be another place for dinner?' she asked as Mel walked to the door.

'No, no, he's in a hurry,' the doc replied.

The response was a little quick to Mel's way of thinking, so he gave Willow a wounded smile and stepped out onto the porch. He heard the desert crickets and smelled the night blossoms, then took a deep breath. In darkness, the town looked less bleak, less faded. Night-time created a flattering cloak, making places like Polvo Gris look no worse than anywhere else.

He crossed the street and went back to Marcella's Quarter. He indicated a bottle of forty-rod whiskey from the shelf along the back bar and paid the barkeep four dollars. He remembered hearing Chief Josef Fish once tell his father, 'Whiskey make rabbit hug bear.' He smiled favourably at the saw, and puffed his cheeks doubtfully at the thought of what might happen if he had a drink with Budge Miner. He left the saloon and turned into the side street, doubtfully made his way to Bill Frater's livery.

He gave the stableboy a dollar and led his grey out front and saddled it. Five minutes later, still uncertain if he was right or wrong, wise or foolish, he rode out into the main street, headed west toward Selwyn Church's homestead.

*

Doc McLane slumped in his porch chair and heaved a long sigh of relief. Willow Legge leaned against the porch rail, studying him closely as he lit one of his cigaritos.

'Are you going to tell me what you're up to?' she asked.

'I'm not up to anything,' he replied, with a barely visible shake of his head.

'Oh yes you are. I've known you too long not to know when there's something devious going on in that head of yours. The hours I've spent listening to men's imaginings. I recognize the look. Nine times out of ten there was a woman involved. You're not the only one concerned about the girl, you know.'

'Most of those men you're talking of were dying, Willow. They needed those thoughts to know they were still living. Anyway, I got us into this problem, it's up to me to get us out . . . me and Reba Church, that is. You stick to looking after my patients and the house, Willow. Leave the other stuff to me.'

'Hmm. I'll wager it's the "other stuff" that's got you into whatever trouble you're talking about,' Willow continued with her concerns. 'You're involved in something you should have stayed away from – something or some*one*.'

'What *are* you going on about, Willow?'

'The Spool foreman, Budge Miner. He's obviously no match for that young man. But to a silly, meddling old sawbones? Tell me you're not involved in something you shouldn't be, Doc . . . please.'

'You reckon I should let her ride out to Selwyn's place on her own?' McLane suggested, veering away from Willow's question. 'You saw how distraught she was when we brought her in, didn't you? Good God, Willow, she fainted at the sight of an ordinary fist-fight.'

'I think it was more than that,' Willow said. 'And I can see how you'd want to help her. You're bored and you want some excitement. But what you're actually getting is . . . big trouble.'

'I'm a doctor, Willow. That makes me part of the real world, not someone who stands and watches,' McLane answered back as Willow walked away. He knew he could depend on her. He'd known it from the time they'd walked from the carnage of war and decided to travel west. They'd first met at Chickamauga, when she'd worked alongside the field surgeons as a volunteer nurse.

Moving off the porch, McLane walked across his small front yard. Reba Church had remained in his front room. She hadn't shown any inclination to leave the house or even talk to anyone. Not that that bothered the doc. Getting justice for Selwyn Church or getting punishment with the Casper Spool hands did. And to that end, he wanted Mel Cody out on the Church place.

He stood by his picket fence and considered another smoke. He took a few breaths of the cool night air. Looking at the lamps that shone from the buildings along the main street he heard wild shouts from Marcella's Quarter, both inside and out. He thought about the old days when towns like Polvo Gris had been open, neighbourly places with no man or family down on their luck, no man as wealthy and dangerously influential as Casper Spool.

He considered the trouble he'd caused Brett Vaughn and decided to take a stroll to the jailhouse. The sheriff sat moodily at his desk building a low stockade with shotgun cartridges. McLane grunted out a welcome and pulled the checkerboard out from under Vaughn's hat. He arranged the well-worn pieces.

Vaughn challenged him with a look and watched him make the first move on the board. 'A whiskey a game,' he said, and went for his pipe.

'Two,' said the old doctor and leaned over the board with eager resolve.

'So much for the early dinner,' Willow said when Doc McLane returned two hours later.

'Yeah, sorry, Willow. I got caught up winning me a half bottle of whiskey,' he said, unbuttoning his coat.

'Well, while you've been doing that, Reba's got herself up and about. She's asking for you. Looks like she's shook off the worst. She's back in the kitchen, eating, now.'

He found Reba sitting at the kitchen table. She

had a bowl of broth that looked untouched cooling before her. She looked up when he came in and gave him a reserved smile.

'I'm sorry for the trouble I've caused you. Willow made this for me, but I can't—'

McLane interrupted, drawing up a chair. 'Appetite'll come with the first mouthful, and it's no trouble. I don't do much that I don't want to anymore. And if there *is* any trouble, believe me, it ain't started yet.'

'Hmm,' Reba said, not picking up on McLane's forewarning. 'My uncle told me very little about the town or his life here. After pa's death he just wrote and said to come on out. It took me nearly three months to tidy up pa's affairs though.'

'You lost your pa as well?' Doc asked, grimacing.

Reba nodded and gave the broth a stir.

The doctor gave her wrist a short understanding grasp. 'If there's any truth in trouble coming three times, I'd stay right here, young lady,' he said thoughtfully. 'If there's anything headed your way, meet it head-on. So, stay; open a new chapter in your life.'

Reba looked intent. 'What am I supposed to do? I'm capable enough, but I don't have the money or the knowledge to go into business. I wouldn't know where to start.'

'You know nothing of ranch work?'

Reba shook her head. 'I ordered some mail-order

seeds once. My pa . . . family ran a shop, a draper's.'

'I see,' he said, appreciating the degree of amuse-
ment in her reply. 'Well it ain't all that challenging if
you've got a head on you and an expert hand. Selwyn
had himself a decent spread. It's three hours west of
here – not big, but the land's pretty. There's good
water and fat grass on the slopes. I'd say there was
some . . . err . . . civic improvements needed, but you
ain't inherited a pig in a poke, Reba.'

'I told you, my background's frills and furbelows.
Besides, I don't take easily to horses and cattle. I
don't like the way they look at you . . . big ugly
brutes.'

'In a lot of ways, cattle and horses are about the
same as people out here, Reba. You treat 'em right
and they'll line up for you.' McLane went to his top
pocket for a cigarito but changed his mind.

'You can smoke if you want. I don't mind. I'm used
to it,' Reba said.

'No, it's all right. Willow don't like it.' He patted
her arm reassuringly with a nervous little grin.
'Anyway, your problem ain't so great. I've sent a man
out to look after things. He's a rough diamond but
there's a charm about him. He won't let you down
either.'

'He'll be the hired hand, will he?'

'Yeah. You'll need someone to keep the fences in
order, chop wood, do some round-up and branding
work. You know, that sort of thing.'

'I can only guess, I'm afraid. You've been so kind, I—'

McLane interrupted again, cutting off her gratitude. 'I don't know much about Selwyn's finances,' he said, 'but he never had any loans that I know of. Well, nothing big enough to cause him any hardship. As I said, the place is probably run down a bit, but I reckon he was making out fair enough. I'm sure you won't have much of a problem there.'

Reba took a mouthful of chicken broth and sipped wistfully. McLane coughed and rose from the table. He'd have been tempted by the girl, a few years ago. But he'd already found Willow by then, so it never would have been anything more.

'I'd like for you to stay here the night,' he said, relieved that Reba hadn't asked who he'd sent out to the ranch. 'In fact, as your doctor, I'd prescribe it. Then sometime tomorrow we'll see what the bank's got your uncle down for, eh? See if there's any more surprises for you. Maybe the day after, we can ride out and you can see what you've become the owner of.'

Reba put the spoon back in the bowl and McLane knew he was getting ahead of himself, had said too much. But he thought it a good sign that she didn't appear to be interested in any gain from her uncle Selwyn's death.

He bade her goodnight then, went back to the front porch and finally drew out the smoke he'd been wanting. He listened to the breeze soughing through the chaparral. All that fuss and he still hadn't had his dinner! As his belly grumbled he inhaled deeply on his cigarito. He hoped that out of the debris of one long day, a better morning would follow.

8

'You bring him closer, so I can get a good look at him.' Casper Spool stamped down off his veranda to glare at Miles Beckman.

Ever since Felix Chelloe had reported back to him about the trouble in town, Spool had been keen to learn more of Selwyn Church's killing. The old man had held a section of land which spiked upwards into his already vast range and refused to sell. Spool had therefore considered his neighbour to be little more than an irksome sodbuster.

Beckman attempted to hold the reins as Miner climbed from his saddle and got a kick for it. Then he offered an assist to the house.

'Get your ham fists off me,' Miner said, shoving him away. The big man braced himself on unsteady legs and took a step onto the broad veranda. He gave Beckman a rich curse and brushed past him up into the house. Spool was on the verge of shouting his

71

foreman down when he saw the extent of Miner's beating. He sucked in his breath at the overall bruising across Miner's face – the raw, puffed-up mouth and the bloodied nose.

Miner limped on into the house. Spool turned on Beckman. 'What the hell happened? It looks like he ran into the Pacific Flyer.'

'I'll let *him* tell it,' Beckman said thickly, and led the two horses off. But he'd not got far when Spool shouted after him.

'Hold up, Miles. Where's Stan?'

'He can tell you that as well,' Beckman muttered over his shoulder.

'I'm asking you, goddamnit.'

'He's dead. Now, if you don't mind, Mr Spool, my mouth feels like it's got a burning log in it, an' I'm kind-of tired. It's been one hell of a day.'

Spool glared furiously as Beckman started off again toward the corral. He was about to shout again, but thought better of it. Instead he hurried into the big day room to find Miner standing with his back to the wall and a glass of Kentucky bourbon in his hand.

'I'm so sorry, Budge,' Spool remarked acidly. 'That was thoughtless of me. I should have said, "Make yourself at home, pour yourself something from my liquor cupboard!"' Warily, the rancher eyed his foreman. 'Felix said Stan killed Selwyn Church. He also said there weren't any trouble with Brett Vaughn or any other townfolk. Beckman says for you to tell me the rest of what happened. Did Felix tell me true, Budge?'

'It's true,' Miner said bluntly.

Spool strode across the room, filled himself a glass of the bourbon and turned back to Miner.' Did you have anything to do with the Church killing?'

'Some.'

'If you don't give me more than that, Budge, you'll end up a range bum in these parts,' Spool threatened.

Miner pushed himself away from the wall he was leaning against. He took a deep, laboured breath. 'You already been told. Stan shot the old man. Vaughn couldn't do much about it. But what you don't know is that while we was talking to Church about him rustling your beeves—'

'What? What do you mean, rustling my beeves?' Spool barked.

Miner raised his eyebrows in a pained expression. 'Yeah. We followed the sign. He had a herd of thirty-five, forty steers. They were bunched in a pole corral at the bottom of the south slope of his spread. We caught up with him in town . . . asked him about it. I figure he panicked . . . went for his gun.'

'Who was it did the asking?' Spool asked.

'Me.'

Spool swore violently. 'Why the hell didn't you ride back here? You know how I feel about cattle-stealing. This far from town about the only law we can count on is our own, and imposed by me.'

'I know that but there weren't time,' Miner said. 'If that sign had . . . got windblown, there'd be no proof. Anyway, I only meant to rough him up a bit, get him to squawk his guilt.'

Spool shook his head slow, and incredulous, 'Did he do that to you, Budge? Was it him that gave you that beating?' Spool held out his glass to indicate the man's damaged face.

Miner held the back of his hand tentatively under his nose. 'No, it weren't Church. That was Melvin Cody.'

'Cody? Who the hell's he?'

'A drifter. He happened by. He got the drop on me . . . got stuck in before I could get myself together.'

'Yeah, and Stan?'

'Stan killed Church. Cody killed Stan.'

Spool gaped. 'I don't think I want to know the whole of this story, Budge. You're telling me that you and Miles *and* Stan got jumped by a drifter who just happened by?' he cracked.

'I said he got the drop on us. He ain't no normal drifter either. Not the kind we see in these parts. He looked like he was a . . . I dunno, not Mex, maybe one of them mestizos. Mean eyes and cold-blooded. I was going after him, but Vaughn stepped in. But no matter, I'll take care of him, soon as I'm right in the saddle again.'

CODY'S FIGHT

'I'm sure you will, Budge,' Spool mocked.

Miner's eyes narrowed in resentment. 'Ease off, Casper,' he said flatly. 'You weren't there. You don't know how it was set up. We got your goddamn beeves back, an' another rustler's kicking up brush. As soon as I can, I'm going after this Melvin Cody.'

'When's that then?' Spool asked.

'Sun-up tomorrow. Meantime, I'll get a slab of meat an' some salt on these wounds. And this time, I won't be involved in any ringster stuff. I'm talking lead.'

Spool finished his drink. He put down his glass heavily, signalling their talk was over. 'You do whatever you think's best, Budge. But now I'm kind-of curious. I think I'll take me a ride into town to see our good sheriff. Find out what's going on . . . see what he's up to.'

Miner finished his drink, and walked tiredly across the room. He stopped near the open door. 'No, Casper,' he said with an edge of unease. 'Leave it to me. I know what to do . . . and who to do it to. That's what you pay me for. Shouldn't take me more'n a day.'

Spool nodded and followed Miner onto the veranda. Miner had been hurt bad, but he'd seen many men who'd been beaten in fights before – seen a lot of it in a mirror when he was making his mark in Polvo Gris. He cursed quietly, and wondered about the man who was calling himself Melvin Cody.

Miles Beckman was brushing his horse when Miner entered the barn.

'I told Spool that Cody got the drop on me,' Miner said.

Beckman kept on brushing. 'That's right, Budge,' he agreed. 'I mean, there's no one going to believe otherwise, is there? If that's how you want it to be told?'

'It is. First thing, you and Felix get to that low country an' clean it out. Take them beeves down to the wash an' leave 'em there. They won't go far.'

'What about you?' Beckman asked anxiously.

'I got something to attend to. I ain't letting no drifter beat the stuffing out of me an' walk away. You just tell the men we was jumped . . . never had a chance. You hear me, Miles?'

'Yeah, I got the picture, boss,' Beckman said.

9

Sunlight reached the town, sought the blistered sur-
faces of its clapboard walls, and brightened the
dullness of the alleys and side streets. Eventually,
Polvo Gris was only a yellow break from the timbered
greenness that bent around Eagle Tail Mountains.
An outcast from the dog pack lay in the dust. It
panted slightly and rose on its front legs, too uncomfortable to stay in the rising sun – but fell back again,
too lazy to move. A rider came along the main street,
threw a package into the doorway of the boarding-
house and rode on. A storekeeper swept the litter of
his shop onto the boardwalk. On the steps of
Marcella's Quarter, a grizzled old man sat. He was
half-keeled over, not quite fallen, and he had both
eyes shut. In the narrow street alongside, a woman
threw a pail of water up over Bill Frater's livery stable
sign.

Sitting on his porch, Doc McLane saw Budge

Miner making his way up the street. When he passed Marcella's and headed on toward the north end of town, the doc eased himself from his chair and walked to his front gate. Then he hurried along the boardwalk until he reached the side street where Selwyn Church had met his death. Miner was only fifty or so yards ahead of him, and still riding slowly.

McLane turned into the lane and jogged in a staggered loop through sheds and workshops until he came to the rear door of the jailhouse. Calling for the sheriff, he thumped on the heavy slabs of pine. 'Brett. It's me, George. Open up, I got something to tell you.'

The door creaked open a few moments later and Vaughn frowned out at him. The doc didn't bother to make his way into the jailhouse, just said urgently: 'Miner's riding in. He's coming this way, and I reckon we know what for.'

Brett Vaughn squeezed his eyes shut for a troubled moment. 'Hold up, George,' he started, but McLane cut him short.

'He's almost here, Brett. Shut up an' listen to me, will you? I got young Mel Cody to ride out to the Church spread. Someone's got to be there, if only to protect the girl . . . Reba. There's likely to be trouble, we know that. I been mulling over what Miner and them cowhands had to say about Selwyn stealing their cows. Well that ain't so . . . can't be. So, who was

78

it moved those cattle onto his land, eh? Who was it, gave Miner the chance to make the accusation?'

'How the hell would I know?' Vaughn rumbled impatiently. 'An' how come you got so involved? You said he's here and headed this way, so make your point fast, George.'

'Never mind me. My involvement ain't important. If it weren't Selwyn, who was it? But right now, even that don't matter. You got to get us time, Brett. You got to get Cody some time.'

The sheriff's brows arched and he puffed, tugged at his loose belt. 'What in the blazes you up to, Doc? Time . . . what the hell you want *time* for? By Big Lucy, if you're putting those goddamn boots of yours into—'

McLane banged the flat of one hand against the door frame. 'I said to listen, Brett. Miner must be just pulling up outside right now. Whatever you say, don't let on where Cody has gone. I got a bad feeling it matters . . . that we all need time. There's something real damn wrong about Selwyn getting shot the way he was. Just tell Miner that Mel Cody went on his way. Just leave it at that.'

Both men heard the pounding on the front door of the jailhouse. McLane nodded his urgent encouragement at Vaughn. 'Please, Brett. Just do it.' Then he pushed the back door open and left before Vaughn could argue further.

*

79

Vaughn swore, stuffed the tail of his shirt into his pants, and tugged at his belt again. Then he unlocked the front door to let in the Spool foreman.

In the bright, slanting light, Miner's face looked a lot worse than he remembered from the day before. It had matured badly. His left eye was almost closed, the flesh across his cheeks, his mouth and nose, were deeply coloured and swollen.

'What do you want, Miner?' Vaughn asked.

'Cody,' the Spool ramrod said. 'You can back him or me; don't matter much. Just find him . . . tell him.'

'Ride away, Miner, before I get to thinking lawful stuff. Busting in here with your threats an' demands. Who the hell do you think you are?'

'The man who's come for Cody,' Miner told him thickly. 'You just stay out of my way, Sheriff. This is between me an' him.'

'Seems like most folk are telling me what to do,' Vaughn snapped back. 'Shame I'm such an ornery old cuss.' He reached for his gunbelt and buckled it around his spreading middle. Then he pushed past Miner and went to sluice water over his face in a corner basin. 'Wouldn't you just love to be able to do this,' he said, towelling himself roughly. 'Now why don't you just settle down? Maybe you was asking for all you got, Miner.'

'I came looking for Cody, Vaughn. Either you go get him or I find him myself. Either way you'll be burying him.'

Vaughn hung the towel on a peg, put his hat on. He smiled thinly. 'You considered that maybe you ain't up to taking him?'

Miner swore, drew his gun in a fast, smooth motion and actioned the hammer.

Vaughn's gun hand dropped instinctively, but he left his gun holstered. 'Jesus, you should be milling with them stolen cows. You think acting the gunny is enough to kill Melvin Cody? You really are more stupid than you look, Miner, an' right now that's saying something.'

'He jumped me from behind. That's how he managed to take me.'

'Rubbish. You came at him like a riled greenhorn. He stepped away then came back an' beat you to a pulp. *That's* how it was.'

Miner released the hammer of his Colt. 'I'm sick of talking. I want Cody, so if you want to see it done fair, you best lead the way, Sheriff.'

'I ain't leading you anywhere. There's no point,' Vaughn said easily.

'You're staying out of it, then?'

'Yeah, sure I am. Don't figure on riding no hundred miles or so just for the hell of it.'

Miner inclined his head, looked at him with his good eye. 'What're you talking about?'

'Cody quit town last night.'

Miner swore. 'When?'

'Smack on sundown. I reckon with him riding all

night on that grey of his, he could be a fair way across the Yuma Desert . . . if he went that way, that is. If he took the Casa Grande trail he'd be near the Cactus Plain.' Vaughn grinned mischievously. 'Of course, he could be building himself a smoke on top of Standup Rock. Then again, if he went—'

'Shut it, Vaughn. Shut your goddamn mouth.' Miner, infuriated, thrust his gun back into his holster. He touched his sore, split lips with the tips of his fingers, took off his hat and rubbed a hand through his hair. 'Which way *did* he go?'

'Now that I didn't see, friend.'

'You saw. You just ain't telling.'

Vaughn grinned widely at him. 'That's for me to know, Miner. But if you want some advice? Go home and count your blessings. Now if you don't mind, I got another day to start, an' I don't want you cluttering up my office. Unless you figure on spending time in one of these cells?'

Miner held the sheriff with a steely glare, then heeled about and stomped out onto the boardwalk. He looked thoughtfully up and down the street, then made it along to Frater's stable. The boy remembered Mel Cody all right, had taken a dollar off him. He confirmed that Cody had taken his horse just after sundown the previous evening, saddled it himself and ridden out.

Miner went back to his own horse and swung stiffly into the saddle. After giving Brett Vaughn another hard look as the lawman watched him from the jail-house, he kicked his mount into a trot and rode from town.

10

Melvin Cody forded Dog Creek for the first time, took a short rest, and resumed his way. The Buckskin Mountains broke into long slopes where lush grassy meadows lay alternately with finger-shaped washes. An hour later, below the pine and spruce, he found the creek again, as Doc McLane told him he would. He put his grey on picket in a small flat of grass and made a meal of two dough-god biscuits and creek water. A small, chill wind moved against him and he drew his blanket in, sat and watched the sun break.

At this hour, the air was thin and clear when Mel rose the strike of his spur on a creekside rock and ran a sharp echo along the edge of timber. Shielding his eyes with his hat, Mel wondered if he was anywhere near where his father had once stood, wondered if it was the picture he'd had in mind when he'd said, 'Look to the country about, son.'

Twenty minutes later, using a broken wheel spoke,

Mel kicked away two aggressive geese while he levered open the back door of Selwyn Church's house. He went into the low-ceilinged building with his stomach churning at the smell, reached for the first window and pushed it open. Then he opened all the windows in the other rooms and the front door.

As fresh air cleared the rooms, he had time to notice the old Hawken rifle in its rack above the lintel. Selwyn's soiled work-clothes were piled in a heap on the floor. An assortment of dirty pans and plates were stacked high on a table. There was a basin of murky water standing in a bowl and an iron pot that contained something that smelled bad. A side of bacon was hanging from a rafter, shiny and beginning to sour. None of it was that unusual: just everyday chores that Selwyn would have eventually gotten round to.

Mel cut down the flitch, gathered the obvious unwanted rubbish and took it all out back. He got some dry leaves and sticks and made a fire of the waste heap. He watched it burn before going back to get the dead man's clothes and other flammable bits and pieces. He drew some water from the well and tipped away the foul, standing juices. Then he went across a small clearing to Selwyn's barn.

The barn was about in the same mess as the house and reeked of soiled straw and horse piss. A few sacks of grain had been roughly split, the contents scattered along the fronts of the two horse stalls. Two saddles hung on wall hooks but it looked like only one was useable. The spread had been running down and, like a lot of settler folk, Selwyn Church had been chary of discarding anything that had some mileage left in it.

One of the horse corrals had a broken rail, another, fallen poles, but generally they were solid enough. Mel unsaddled his grey and turned it into the yard after fixing a low sapling bar. Then he hefted his possessions up into the barn loft. He worked for half an hour before he had a bagged-straw mattress and his spartan belongings piled into an empty fruit box. When he was satisfied that he was sorted out, he saddled up an inquisitive cow pony that came to greet him and went to inspect the rest of the Church property.

He got an impression of the land and its bound-aries, made mental notes of the damaged fences, how the creek was silting up downstream. A long hour later back at the ranch house, he took an early pull of his whiskey and contemplated the work ahead.

Mel figured it would take him five, maybe six days to get the house and its immediate surroundings fixed and tidied. After an unhurried smoke he took off his shirt and grabbed an axe he'd found in a lean-to tool-shed. He went onto the slopes and, in the hot afternoon sun, he swung at timber. It was a task he knew and was skilful at. He soon had cut enough to make fence posts and repair the barn and corrals.

That night he slept a weary sleep, and was up at first light. He started work on the north wall of the barn, remaining at the job until the noon heat drove him upstream into the icy creek water. He rested for an hour and ate some more of his biscuits. This time though, he had them with wild onions and a goose egg. He found an unopened tin of condensed milk and some sugar and he made strong, sweet coffee. After his accustomed smoke, he started work again. Then at sundown, with his muscles jingling with the work of sawing and hammering, he stretched out on the porch to survey his labour. He watched the geese go for a lone heron probing the rushes for frogs. He was tired, but alert and more content than he'd been the night before.

He was sipping his whiskey from a tin mug when two riders came up from the creek. He sat in the dark shadows, only the intermittent glow from the tip of his cigarette marking his presence. He silently placed the mug at his feet and pinched out the tip of his smoke, then sat unmoving.

The riders came straight for the house. The geese hissed an alarm, but knew enough to stay away from the horses' hoofs.

'Ol' Selwyn liked his grog. We might get ourselves lucky this night,' one of the men said, as they pulled their horses up.

They were swinging from their saddles when Mel

walked slowly to the doorway. Mel was light-footed, but his footfall made an ominous noise in the night silence. The two men stopped suddenly as they approached the porch steps and dropped hands to their side arms.

'Don't touch them guns,' Mel demanded, remembering that he'd wound his waistband around his Colt and left it in the melon box. He stretched an arm up until he felt the breech of the Hawken above the door.

Alarmed and surprised, the men did as they were told. They looked hard at each other and backed off a pace.

'Who the hell's speaking, mister? This is Selwyn Church's place,' the same man said. 'We're neighbours, an' we know he ain't here.'

'But you think his grog might be,' Mel said.' You were about to steal a dead man's bottle. Now the two of you move real slow while I get myself a little lamp going here. I wouldn't want to put a hole in someone's belly's when I meant to take their legs out, now would I?'

'Who the hell are you?' the other man growled.

'I'm the hired hand,' Mel told him.

'Selwyn lived here alone. He never took on no hired hand.'

'I'm working for his niece,' Mel said flatly. 'You staying on for that drink?'

The two men looked at each other again. In the

shadows they could see Mel's raised arm or guess where he had his hand. After a few moments' thought, they backed toward their horses.

Mel remained very still. He could just see them climb aboard their mounts. 'If you two ever come back, make sure it's daylight. I got an aversion to night riders . . . might just turn real un-neighbourly.'

The man who'd spoken first sniffed and hawked. 'We'll be back, daylight or not. I'm going to get you checked out, mister.'

Mel drew back the hammer of the big-bored rifle, flinched as the deadly, metallic snap splintered the night. 'I've changed my mind,' he said. 'Get off this land, an' don't ever come back.'

The riders turned their horses. Mel watched until the ribbon of light broke as they crossed the creek downstream. They must have headed east, in the general direction of Casper Spool's land.

Casper Spool looked hard at his two hired hands. 'So, the old coot has himself a niece, does he?'

'That's what he said, Mr Spool. Said that was who he was working for.'

'And who exactly was he?'

'Hired hand, he said. It weren't that friendly a meeting.'

Spool frowned. 'Well, what did he look like?'

'It was dark, Mr Spool. You can't—'

'So you let him sweet-talk you? You never thought

to bust him, just got your asses safely back here. Is that it?'

One of the two men showed surprise. 'Hell, Mr Spool, if you've ever heard the sound of a big rifle being cocked a few feet from your face in the dark, you don't stand around arguing.'

Spool sighed wearily. In the last few days he'd realized just what a seedy and disorderly outfit he'd got on the payroll. Not so long ago he'd had good reliable men: rawhiders who knew their place, the way of things. But now he reckoned he was employing treacherous men who were getting the nod from Budge Miner rather than himself.

He looked up. In the light from his house lamps he saw Miles Beckman and Miner walking toward him. 'These boys say there's a gun staked out on the Church place, Budge. Do you know anything about it?'

Miner shook his head. 'Nope. I was in town most of yesterday. Today I been working the bottom country with Felix and Miles.' He turned to the two men. 'A gun, you say? Who the hell was he?'

'They didn't see him because of the dark, and they didn't get his name because he didn't tell,' Spool mocked. 'All they did was ride away and come straight back here.' Spool looked out at the two men, but he didn't know them well, didn't even know their names. He was wearying of the task, of even giving Miner the responsibility of hiring new hands for the herding season.

'Tomorrow, we'll ride over and take a look at this feller,' he told Budge firmly. 'It's no secret I want that land. I suppose I'll have to go through Selwyn's niece to get it. We'll leave at sun-up, might even go on into town if the deal means me seeing her personal.'

Spool turned back into the house. Miner followed, but the ranch owner was expecting it and closed his front door quickly. Miner pulled up short and his beaten face took on a heavier colour. For a short moment, his eyes bored into the solid timber. Then he turned, and strode from the porch. He hurried across the yard with Miles Beckman close on his heels.

'Looks like you got the ticket away from Mr Spool's gang, Budge,' he said.

'Shut it,' Miner snarled.

Outside the bunkhouse he turned sourly to Beckman. 'Tomorrow, you an' Felix get that section cleared out. Drive the cattle down the wash. I'll go with Spool, try an' keep him busy 'til we get them beeves on the run for Yuma. I want no mistakes, Miles. Anybody gets wind of what's going on, tell 'em to see me. You're just carrying out ramrod's orders.'

'We already got nigh-on three hundred head, Budge,' Beckman contended.

'So? We want another hundred, maybe two if we can get 'em. I'm not pulling out short if I can help it. Spool can afford it.'

Beckman said nothing more, but stood watching in the looming darkness as Miner turned back toward the cookhouse.

Miner spent a quarter-hour tenderly bathing his face with brine water before he returned to the bunkhouse. His whole body hurt, and his mind turned to murderous thoughts. First, he was going to relieve his boss of four to five hundred head of good cattle. Then he'd drift, search out Melvin Cody, maybe even kill him.

11

Reba rose early. For two days, she'd ventured no further than the outskirts of Polvo Gris. Doc McLane had introduced her to many of the townspeople. Now, walking with the doctor to the livery stable, she was taking a different view on the town.

Her first reaction to it had been one of abject horror. From the window of the stagecoach, she'd seen no redeeming features to the stark frontier town – nothing that could possibly appeal to her. Things seemed a little different now that she'd spent a few days here. The people who claimed friendship with her uncle she'd found kindly and sympathetic to her predicament. Perhaps the town was, after all, a likely place for her to settle.

Eager nervousness gripped her as she climbed into the rig that McLane had hired to go and visit the Church spread. Spending time with the doctor and Willow Legge had given her something to think about. Now that she owned something, she could consider things other than the fripperies of the drapery.

A more optimistic Reba Church drove out that morning with George McLane. As they waved to Willow and left the northern end of town, the sun burst through, lifting itself high across the distant Cactus Plain.

McLane waved an arm at the land ahead of them. 'I keep thinking of this as Selwyn's place, but I guess it's yours now, Reba. Yeah, it's your place. It's set up high on the lush slopes, with Dog Creek running through it, and plenty of timber. Was a while back that I spent some time out there . . . doctor's rounds, you know. When that big sun hits the trees . . .' McLane stopped for a moment. 'Oh yeah, it was pretty, all right. Makes me wonder why I spend so much time in town.'

'Because that's where the people are . . . who need looking after, I guess,' Reba offered. 'It must be good to have so many close friends. To have won their respect.'

'Hmmm. There's times when I think I'd rather have won something else. An argument maybe? A seat on the State Legislature?'

'You're unhappy in Polvo Gris?'

McLane shrugged and flicked the reins. 'Weary. Bored to tears, more like it. And winning their respect's not quite what it seems. I know so many secrets and been told so much in confidence, it's difficult for most folk to be anything *but* respectful.'

'What did you know about my uncle?' Reba asked, before McLane got to be too sentimental or personal.

'You're not going to like it, girl,' McLane started uncertainly. 'But then again it's only an accusation.'

'What accusation?'

McLane watched the track ahead of them as they took a long shallow bend. He let the horse settle into an even gait. He pulled one of his cigaritos, thought about it and put it back. 'Selwyn was accused of being a rustler . . . a cattle thief.'

'I do know what a rustler is, Doc. Who accused him of being one?'

'A neighbour of his. Yours now.'

As if by instinct, Reba's mind went back to her arrival in town, the fighting in the street. 'You can tell me, Doc. I'm not for swooning . . . not anymore.'

'Budge Miner was one of them. They claimed Selwyn stole some of your neighbour's cattle . . . had 'em corralled on his land.'

'What neighbour?' Reba asked curtly.

'Casper Spool. Selwyn called them all liars. Miner tore into him. That was when our young Geronimo came along . . . stopped him being beaten up bad.'

'What Geronimo? What do you mean?'

'I mean, Melvin Cody,' he said sourly. 'Sorry, the tag's not funny and it's nowhere near accurate either.

95

He's just got some Indian blood in him,' The doc took a deep breath, 'And I really have got to tell you about him . . . very soon. Anyway, old Selwyn went for his gun. The shame of it was, he was killed before he could do any damage. Even the sheriff agreed.'

The colour drained from Reba's face and she held her hands tight as McLane continued.

'The upshot was your poor uncle lying dead in the street, and Mel Cody keeping the curs at bay until the sheriff arrived to jail him.'

'He was the man in the street, wasn't he?'

'That was him – the last one left standing,' McLane grinned, almost chuckled.

'And he was jailed for helping my uncle? An old man who was bullied and outnumbered?' Reba asked.

'Yeah, that's the cruel irony. But that's not the fault of Brett Vaughn, Reba . . . not totally. Miner accused Cody of being in cahoots with Selwyn, so he reckoned he had to do something.'

Reba screwed up her face. 'What?' she said, dumbfounded. 'The sheriff just "reckoned he had to do something"? Didn't he know Selwyn?'

'I was getting to that, Reba. I'd seen this stranger riding into town earlier – about an hour later than Selwyn came by. I wanted the boy let out. Of course he weren't in cahoots with Selwyn. They'd never even seen each other before.'

'How did he get out then . . . Melvin Cody?'

'Well that's the curious thing. Miner must have

come up with something. It doesn't make much sense for what happened next.'

Reba's concern showed, but she kept her silence.

'After he was let out, Mel came down the street, headed for Marcella's,' the doctor went on, 'and one of Miner's men dropped a rope around his shoulders. He got dragged off the boardwalk, near pulled under the stage you were on.'

'Yes, I saw that part of the story and what happened next.'

'Yeah, well then Rourke came along. He was gunning for Mel. There was no other way.'

'Why doesn't that surprise me?' Reba said scathingly.

'What Mel Cody did lets him fight another day. And that's what will happen.'

'Why?'

McLane stared into the distance as he answered. 'Because it's him that's out at the ranch. Your ranch.'

'I should have guessed. The good doctor's got me a gunman to chop firewood and mend fences.'

'He's the man that sided with your uncle, Reba. He could have walked away. He didn't believe he had a choice. He's a good man.'

'Yes, I know. I'm sorry, Doc. I didn't mean he wasn't.'

'Forget it.'

'Do you think there'll be more fighting on my land?'

97

'Out here, Reba, you've got to be ready for most things. I guess gunfights are just the worst of them.' As he spoke, McLane drew rein and pointed ahead. 'Just down there. Along the slope and we cut the creek again, then it's your land, Reba Church. Why don't you sit quiet now . . . take it in and just see if this isn't God's own country.' McLane smiled warmly. 'It's worth fighting for. Selwyn knew it . . . wouldn't be pushed off.'

But Reba couldn't see much of the country that stretched out before her. She was fighting it well, keeping her emotions in check. From what the doctor had said, she was employing the man who'd shot someone dead in the middle of Polvo Gris's main street. It was true that Mel Cody had gone to the aid of her uncle. But if Cody stayed on her ranch, she too would be involved in neighbour trouble. She didn't know how to resolve the problem with the well-meaning doctor.

The rig worked its way across the shallow bed of the creek crossing, went rolling easily up the long slope. Through the noises of harness and rig Reba heard the carried sound of a hammer smacking into clout nails. Then, all of a sudden the house was before them. The mid-morning sun touched the grass and beamed into the pine and spruce that edged the slopes around the compact building. In spite of her troubled thoughts, Reba couldn't hold back a short intake of breath when she saw the colour and richness of the land.

'Shame it's all got to be spoiled by ugly brutes of cows,' she said.

'Not just the cows,' McLane agreed.

Reba nodded, afraid to look at anything else lest Mel Cody appear. In her imagination, the man who'd tried to save her uncle had now reverted to the war-painted savages she'd encountered in dime novels.

12

'There's our man,' McLane said and pointed off to the left.

Reba tried not to look but found her head coming about anyway. Mel Cody was striding across the long eastern slope, the long heft of an axe in his right hand, his cambric shirt tied loosely around his waist.

Reba tensed. McLane reached across and gripped her arm. 'Cut him some slack,' he said quietly. 'It might not all go as badly as you think.'

Reba shrugged from his touch. 'It already is. I saw his eyes. The memory's come back. I didn't think it would.'

'I told you, he's a good man, Reba. I know it,' McLane said defensively.

'How can you know that? He didn't carry recommendations on him, did he?'

'Not all of us arrive with that, Reba. This is still a frontier, and there's other ways of reading a man. If you'll let me be blunt, ma'am, if you're aimin' to stay, maybe you should look at things as they actually are.' Mel was close now, so he dropped the axe head to the ground and leaned on the heft. As the rig approached, he looked up at Reba and saw her blush of embarrassment.

For Reba Church it was a curiously troubled moment. She was almost instantly moved by the contradiction of what she'd thought and what she saw.

'Hello there, Mel. Miss Church has come to look at the house. You've been working off some aches, I see.'

'Yeah, a few,' Mel agreed, his eyes still on Reba. 'But there's still a heap of work to do.'

'Thank you for what you've done. What there's still to do ... if you're interested ...' Reba found herself saying, albeit haltingly. She tried again. 'If you want the job for longer, I need the help.'

Mel nodded in response. 'I'll thank you for giving me the chance to stay, ma'am. Not for the work, though. I aim to earn my pay,' he said.

McLane grinned indulgently. 'You done good, Mel. But now we got things to talk about.'

'It's going to get real hot out here. Why don't you get Miss Church's luggage, take her into the house, out of the sun an' away from them goddamn geese,' Mel said. 'I had some time an' made me a nest in the barn.'

101

McLane considered Mel's choice of words, thought there might be another problem. He climbed down from the rig and offered a hand to Reba. Despite her obvious reluctance, he led her into the house. He could see she was uneasy and there were bits and pieces for her to look at. He left her there, looking at what could be family mementos, then he returned to catch up with Mel who was lifting a pail of water onto a table outside the barn.

'You don't need to get close to sense the temperature she's blowing, Doc. So what exactly is it you've been telling her about me?' Mel asked.

'She's a draper's daughter, Mel. Young and impressionable too. She's not looked too long into this world. Give her time.'

Mel shook his head. 'She wants no part of this place, an' I reckon you knew it. But you want rid of Budge Miner so much, you ain't going to see it. That's what I think.'

'Yeah, well that's as may be. But if that weren't enough, she lost her pa a few months back. There's no family left.'

Mel held up and stared confusedly at McLane. 'What the hell are you trying to do, then? I thought doctors were supposed to help.'

'They do. And that's exactly what I'm doing. Not just because somebody has to.'

Using both hands, Mel rinsed his face. He rubbed his chest and shoulders, took a deep breath. 'You

102

better tell me, then,' he said, sputtering water.

'Casper Spool has always wanted the tail section of this spread, but Selwyn wasn't interested in selling. So, accepting that Selwyn wasn't a cattle thief . . . which he wasn't, I reckon they killed him for it.'

Mel untied his shirt. 'How would they have got it?' he asked.

'A land sale . . . a settlement of property? I don't suppose there would have been any claim or opposition. But like most of us, Spool never reckoned on a niece turning up.'

'Seems to me you're sending us out along a cracked branch on that reckoning, Doc. What else you got on your mind?'

'Right now? Those two riders,' he said, nodding out at the green pasture.

Mel turned. A rider who was obviously running to fat was nearing the farm, sided by a grim-faced Budge Miner. Mel eyed them for a moment more, then stepped quickly into the barn. When he returned, he'd donned a long skin shirt. The Colt, which he placed on the table behind the water pail, was ready if needed.

'You going to throw pills, or do you prefer that I handle this?' Mel asked.

'I'm plum out of ammo, kid. You're on your own,' McLane said with a friendly grin. 'Let's move to the house to do our talking. That's Casper Spool riding with Miner and he knows better than to harm me. As for you, Mel . . . ?' McLane let the words hang before continuing. 'Let me do the talking, though. Maybe I can work my way round 'em.'

They set off across the yard. Mel swore under his breath in aggravation. Miner and Spool were well out of the timber now and approaching the back of the house. McLane went on, but Mel held his ground. He stared hard at the two riders and saw the angry twitch of Miner's wounded jaw.

Spool gave a sharp signal with his right hand and Miner pulled his horse in behind his boss. Doc McLane stepped out from the front of the house with Reba alongside. She looked straight at Mel, and her eyes blazed when she saw he was now holding the gun down at his side.

Spool and his ramrod reined in, and the rancher removed his hat. He glanced speculatively at Mel before nodding at Reba.

'Ma'am. I guess you'll be Selwyn Church's niece,' he said.

Reba nodded.

Spool gave a fleeting smile. 'I'm Casper Spool,' he said. 'I'm known to the doc here, and vice versa, so we can get settled straightaway. Mine's the land that borders your lower slopes . . . the south boundary beyond the creek. It's regrettable what happened to your uncle, but—'

'Regrettable!' snapped McLane. 'What in the name of God are you talking about? You sent those sons-of-bitches into town to gun down Selwyn. Four of 'em against one old man. Those always the sort of odds you go for, Spool?'

The muscles tightened in Spool's face and Budge Miner shifted in his saddle.

Mel leaned against the low veranda fence, placed his Colt on top of the hand rail. He deftly built himself a cigarette, but his casual stance suggested a man who'd just as soon hold a gun in his hand.

Spool prodded his horse a little closer to McLane. 'This is between me and the girl. Butt out.'

'That's where you're wrong, friend. You see, I'm advising and prescribing for Miss Church. And I will, until she says otherwise,' McLane retorted. 'She doesn't know you, and Selwyn was a friend of long standing. So I'm not going to stand by and let you cheat her out of this ranch or anything else.'

Spool ground his teeth. 'A thousand dollars isn't cheating. That's the deal I had with Selwyn ... the deal he accepted. Now I'm offering fifteen hundred.' Spool looked at Reba and smiled archly. 'If you want to go on living here, that can be arranged. If you want to carry yourself with crops, play around with a horns-an'-bone herd, that can be arranged, too. But there's no percentage in being hasty about a thing like this. You can have until this evening.'

'You're wasting your time, Spool. Yours, mine and hers. So why don't you take that bag of buffalo guts that rode in with you and go home.'

Spool backed up his horse a few paces, and Miner came forward to join him.

'Don't push your luck, ol' feller,' he threatened while taking a quick, sideways glance at Mel.

'Habit from most of a lifetime. It was something I learned at Chickamauga,' McLane told him. 'There was no other way then and no other way now. And talking of those who push their luck, why don't you clear off this land? There's some of us got work to do.'

Mel flicked away his cigarette butt and flexed the fingers of his right hand. He was ready to move. Both Miner and Spool saw the slight movement.

'We taking ultimatums from these two, boss? An ol' quack an' a 'breed drifter?' Miner questioned sourly. 'Why don't we teach 'em a lesson right here . . . deal with the girl after? She looks to me like a filly that don't like heat an' flies bothering her. Reckon she'd prefer town, with its comforts.'

'If the lady wants you to stay, she'll invite you to get down. If not, she won't.' Mel turned to Reba and asked, 'You want 'em to stay, ma'am?'

Reba shook her head slowly. 'No. I would prefer it if they left,' she said.

Mel tensed like a mountain lion and his eyes gleamed. 'You heard,' he said with fearsome menace. 'The lady's given her orders. Now why don't you an' manure-mouth do as the doc suggests, an' ride off?'

'Yeah, why not? It's over, Spool. There's nothing

more for you here,' McLane said, and took Reba's arm, guiding her back along the short veranda. But Reba had begun to tremble at the ultimatums and she stopped when they got to the doorway.

'No,' she protested. 'I want to see what sort of neighbours they really are.' Miner cursed and kicked a heel into the belly of his horse, grabbing for the revolver at his waist.

He'd hardly cleared the leather of his holster before Mel flashed his hand to his own Colt. In an instant, he had the blue steel barrel pointing up into Miner's startled, overwhelmed face.

The blur of movement brought a gasp then a low oath from Spool. 'You're real adept with that gun, Mister Cody. Not your everyday plough-chaser.'

Mel smiled grimly at Miner. 'Yeah I know. Must come as a real surprise. My pa once told me never to pull a gun unless I aimed to use it. He never told me about exceptions, though. I guess I'll have to learn as I go along. You want to risk it, you big, ugly son-of-a-bitch?'

Miner snorted loudly and shifted in his saddle. He was fighting down an urge to rush Mel, but it was a doomed challenge and his shoulders slumped. 'There'll be another time, Cody,' he muttered, drawing his hand away from the holster. 'You ain't finished with me.'

'Clear off,' Mel said. 'If there is a next time, I'll set the geese on you.' He crooked his arm and, against

107

his thumb, opened and closed the forefinger of his right hand, hissed between his teeth in goosey derision.

Mel stood watching as the Spool pair moved off. Not until they disappeared into the first stand of pine did he move away from the house. Without another word from Reba or Doc McLane, he'd heard the front door close. On his way to the barn, his forehead was creased. He knew there was going to be trouble with Miner, but it didn't overly concern him. He was bothered by the opinion Reba Church had formed of him. He was put out because she'd seemed to take it for granted that he'd fight for her. Perhaps he'd have to reconsider his position. He wasn't the only one who could close a door on something he didn't like the look of.

He went into the barn, muttering as he climbed the ladder to his lofty lair.

13

Reba Church ran a finger along a shelf and frowned at the dust.

Watching her, McLane said, 'Selwyn weren't a tidy man, but he had honest values.' Reba didn't say anything, so he went on, 'I'm sorry I took over out there, Reba, but Spool was lying to you. Selwyn didn't make any deal: I know how he felt about this place. There's no way he ever meant to leave it . . . except to you. That makes Spool a liar, and I couldn't let him get away with it.'

Reba walked thoughtfully from the small room. Not a window in the house had curtains to keep out the harsh sunlight. The floor was rough-finished planks, but she doubted if it had ever been washed down or even seen a broom. The air, even for its recent airing, was stale. The light from the window was thick with the glow of rising dust motes.

'At least I can manage the cleaning, if nothing else,' she said, feeling the dirt clinging to her hair. 'It won't be done overnight, though.'

'Does that mean you'll stay?' McLane asked intently. 'Are you taking into account that outburst of mine?'

'I might stay for a month. I had no real plan to sell before I looked the place over, you know, Doc. Uncle Selwyn did write, telling me how wonderful the country was. I wasn't going to sell up before I gave the place, or me, a chance. Even draper's daughters aren't that dim-witted.'

'Hmm, I guess not. What about Mel, then?' Doc asked, uncertainly.

Reba lifted the lid of a blanket box and fingered the contents with a glint of approval. 'Selwyn didn't write me about him,' she said, smiling. 'I really don't know. Giving it some thought is the least I can do, though.'

'Yeah, that's right, Reba,' McLane responded. 'I can only imagine what first impression Mel gave you, but it was me asked him to come out here. In two days he's already got the place part fixed, if you overlook the dust. And I don't think he's going off on a war dance over Miner and Casper Spool. I'd say he acted respectable-like, real committed.'

'Don't get too long on your praise,' Reba suggested. 'He's got doubts.'

McLane laughed scornfully. 'Oh yeah, he's got

them all right. He knows how blood-spilling affects you. No, Reba. He acted just the way I thought he would. He's the man you're looking for right now.'

Reba walked to the door and pushed it fully open. McLane came and stood beside her.

'Give it that month,' he said encouragingly. 'Whatever heaven on earth looks like, this'll be it, believe me. Casper Spool wants to annex it so bad, that must tell you its true worth. You don't have to move, Reba. You got a life right here. A good life.'

'I'd be happier if you knew more about Melvin Cody,' she said.

'Well he's got some rough edges, that's for sure. But you got to admit, he gets things moving. Unless there's some other problem you got concerning him, Reba?'

'I'll be out here on my own. What do you think?' Reba murmured.

McLane gulped and looked out toward the barn. 'I think it's about trust and goodwill. But if it's some other feeling you're worried about, perhaps you should ride out of here right now. I'll take you back to town. You can sell up to Spool, take the coach right back home.'

'Don't be annoyed, Doc,' she said, lowering her head in an attempt to mask the fluster. 'I just need a little more time.'

'Well, Reba, I reckon that's something we're plumb out of.'

111

Reba saw Mel come out of the barn. He led his grey to the corral where he swung up and looked toward the creek. He had a coil of wire slung across his shoulder, a hammer, nails and staples in a saddle-bag.

'Give him a chance,' McLane said. 'He's giving you one. I mean, how much do you need to know about hired help?'

For Reba, the words stung. But McLane was already down the steps, hurrying across the yard.

McLane removed his hat, dabbed at his forehead. 'I reckon I've won her round, Mel,' he said guardedly. 'She was worried you'd be wanting more'n wages.'

Mel's eyes narrowed. 'What's changed her mind?'

'I hinted at bear grease and buffalo blankets. You know, that sort of thing.'

'You done me a favour then?' he said drily.

McLane studied him for a moment then breathed a big sigh. 'That's up to you. I've always believed that opportunity comes to all who work for it.' The doc gestured with his hands. 'So good luck. And watch out for Budge Miner. I noticed he had a hungry gleam in his eye. Even if it was a touch bloodshot.'

He turned and walked away, but Mel called out, 'Hey, Doc. Hold up a minute.'

McLane looked back. 'Yeah?'

'I don't know what you got in mind,' Mel said, 'but it might be best if you stayed away. Miner will make a play, and when he does, I don't want you here. But after, well, I'll be moving on. I ain't having no woman boss.'

McLane gaped at him. 'Why in hell not?' Her dollars are just as good as anyone else's.' Then he thought for a moment. 'Oh yeah, I forgot,' he said, and his face crumpled into a knowing grin. 'There's probably some part of you believes that womenfolk find pleasure in doing the chores. Well, suit yourself, but I reckon you got to leave that way of life behind you, son, and I don't mean no offence.'

'Well there's some taken, Doc.' Mel said. 'But it cuts both ways.'

'Yeah,' McLane replied a little cheerlessly. 'Seems you both got a lot to leave behind . . . a lot of rethinking to do.' He raised a farewell hand, and went back to his rig. Clutching the reins, he watched Mel heel his grey off again, down toward the creek.

He swung the rig around outside the front of the house and called out to Reba. 'You got nothing to worry about except maybe worrying. For the most part, leave him be. He'll keep his own counsel most of the time. If you want me for anything, you know where to find me.' And with that, McLane gave the horse its head back to Polvo Gris.

As soon as Mel was out of sight, Reba walked up to the barn. She saw he had cleaned up, tidied sacks and sorted tack. The ladder to the loft had been fitted with a few new rungs and the north wall had been mended.

Looking up, she saw a shirt flapping in the breeze which came through a high window. She listened for a moment, then climbed up until she could see over the edge of the loft flooring. She saw his straw-bagged bedding, his few personal belongings in the fruit box. On top was the sash that Mel wore around his waist. Fascinated, she took another step upwards. She picked up one end of the sash, ran her thumb across the intricate, coloured glass beads. She was shocked and couldn't believe that a seemingly brutal man could possibly own such an exquisite object.

Surprised at her inquisitiveness, Reba returned quickly to the yard. She looked to where Mel had been riding, then went back to the house and opened one of her two bags. She changed into working clothes and set to on the floorboards.

Mel rode into the yard at sundown. He was tired, encrusted with dried sweat and dust, but he looked quietly satisfied. From a front window where she'd been sitting for some time, Reba saw him pull off his shirt and wash himself down from the water pail outside of the barn. He seemed to glow in the yellow sunset, and for a moment she was curiously moved by the way his wet glossy hair clung to the muscles of his neck. But then she sniffed and turned away to fix up a cold supper. There was chicken, pickled eggs, cheese and a large slice of peach pie, starter food-stuff that Willow Legge had thoughtfully packed into the rig.

As darkness began to settle, Reba lit an oil lamp and a string of happy jack o'lanterns. Instinctively, she started to set out a table, but thought better of it. Instead, she set Mel's meal on a trencher and carried it to the door.

Mel stood in the doorway of the barn, smoking. When he saw her, he tossed the cigarette aside and went forward to meet her. 'I'll bring the plates back in the morning. Thank you, an' goodnight, ma'am,' he said quietly, accepting the tray.

Reba brushed a long strand of dusty hair from her face. She realized she'd not bothered to tidy herself since noon. She was still wearing the clothes she'd last worn when sweeping the stoop of her father's store in Jerome City. As Mel looked at her, she hoped the fading light would disguise the colour in her cheeks.

'Thank you, ma'am,' Mel said again. 'That's real thoughtful. Tomorrow I'll be gone early. The creek needs to be dragged off, where it's silting. If you want me, thump a stick against something. I'll hear it an' come running.' He smiled, then was gone and Reba returned to the house. She sat down and looked at the wedge of cheese, the sliver of pie she'd left herself. As tears of exhaustion welled in her eyes she brushed her hand angrily at a fat blowfly. She started to tremble and felt the crush of isolation and loneliness.

14

Reba was awakened by the sound of the grey's hoof-beats as Mel rode off in the morning. She was surprised to find the light was already creeping around the edges of a blanket she'd pressed into the window frame. Dressing hurriedly, she went to the kitchen and found that he'd already replaced his two supper plates. Somehow she knew they'd be there, but was shocked at discovering that Mel had entered the house while she slept. She moved to the front door, scanned the grass-covered slope, and saw him riding down. Only his head and shoulders were visible above the early, low-curling mist.

Reba's shoulders drooped. She didn't know how to take Mel. She went back to the scullery and ate the food she'd left untouched the night before. She saw the chopped timber he'd piled against the wall just outside the back door, the freshly pumped water in a big pitcher on the table. He'd invaded her privacy, but he was helpful, and that sort of evened things up.

There was still a lot of work ahead, though, and while Reba worked hard all morning, scrubbing, tidying and moving stuff around, she still didn't seem to be achieving much. She found the scattergun above the door and ran the back of her hand along the twin barrels. The stock felt hard and smooth in her grip. Then, curiously frightened, she replaced it and turned away. She made window curtains from the dress she'd travelled in. The main room started to look like someone's home. It wasn't yet hers, and it saddened her to think of her uncle not having much in the way of comforts.

Mel returned at noon. He hitched the grey in the overhanging lee of the barn, flipped his hat over the pommel of the saddle, washed his face and walked to the house. Outside the front door he called out, waiting a moment for Reba to appear in the doorway.

'I let myself in earlier . . . had an egg. I didn't disturb you, did I? I got my own coffee makin's in the barn.'

'No, that's all right. I never heard a thing,' she heard herself saying.

'I got to thinking, though. If you want, you can lay out some jerky for me. Perhaps some bread . . . drippin's, maybe, when you get set up. I can eat in the saddle.'

'That sounds dreadful . . . wouldn't keep a mouse

alive,' Reba said quickly. 'I thought all cowboys ate hugely?'

'I ain't really a cowboy, ma'am. I was brought up on mudfish, nuts an' snake. What I'm asking you for's a real treat.'

Reba looked askance at Mel for a moment, raised her chin and half-smiled. 'I do have a lot to learn, I know,' she said. 'Don't worry, I'll make sure you get well fed.'

'I got to make a pen for them godda— sorry, ma'am. Over the Quill Lakes, there's so many geese, they turn the sky black. But here, you got two of 'em just want to peck me to pieces.'

'Yes, well we can't have that. You do what you think's best. Will you always have to work this long?' Reba asked.

'As long as I'm here, ma'am . . . yes,' Mel said slowly, trying to measure the implication. 'I don't want to burn up in the heat of the day. So for the time being I'll be going out an hour before sun-up. I'll come back at eleven. After a bite, I'll work until the sun starts to drop . . . around four.'

'There's that much to do, is there?'

'Well I sure ain't making it up. The fences come first, I reckon. Most of 'em need tending, an' they won't wait.'

'Yes,' Reba said quietly.

Mel nodded, turned and walked away.

'The pump doesn't work properly,' she called after

him. The words came tumbling, and she realized she must have sounded anxious, as if she wasn't keen to see him leave. She took a breath. 'At the side of the house. There's no draw from the pump. I checked the prime and the pump leather. Could it be the well's run dry?'

'No, ma'am. Not on this slope. It's one of the good things about the place. I'll take a look at it.'

'Thank you. I'll make some food. Will you want to eat it here?'

Mel smiled and pointed to the back of the house. 'I'll be working out there this afternoon. There's some fruit trees need cutting back an' a feeder ditch needs clearing out. Doc McLane said there's a market in town every week. Come the fall, you could make some money selling apples.'

Reba smiled in return and watched Mel go to the trough above which the pump was set up. Then she went straight back to the house and plumped herself into a chair. She knew she should have controlled her emotions better. Mel Cody was the hired help – a man with whom she could never have anything in common. But as soon as she'd thought it, Reba recognized just how wrong she was.

Half an hour later when Reba came out with his food, the trough was filled to overflowing.

'What was wrong?' she asked.

'Nothing much. It just needed fixing,' he said, and thanked her for the trencher.

Again, Reba was perplexed. She felt a curious frustration in the way they conversed.

Mel tugged at the brim of his hat and settled in the shade of a fruit tree circle that Reba's uncle had planted. He was mopping at gravy and contemplating a smoke, when Reba came around the corner of the house with two mugs of coffee. She was only twenty feet from him, was still thinking about what to say, when a bullet spat into the ground between them. At the echoed crack of the rifle, Reba stopped walking, her mouth opened and closed and she dropped the mugs. She made a small, choking cry, looked at Mel, stunned, then started to tremble.

Mel got to his feet and turned in one smooth movement. Reba lifted her hands to her face, took a step backwards. Then a second bullet smashed into the wooden platter, sent Mel's food plate and his fork flying into the air.

Mel swore. Then he yelled at her. 'Get to the house. Go now!'

Reba stood there shaking her head, swaying unsteadily. Mel held out one hand toward her, pointing his gun at the timber where everything appeared normal, unmoving.

'For God's sake, move, woman, or we'll both die out here!' he bellowed, his eyes bright with anger.

Mel's shout shocked Reba from her frozen fear. She turned and fled.

121

As soon as she rounded the corner of the house, Mel made his way through the trees. Running from the orchard and up the grassy slope, he saw Miles Beckman and another rider bearing down on him from the timber stands. He swerved to the left and ran for a big, fallen spruce. He vaulted the tree and rolled down into its dirt-filled depression. Then he quickly regained his footing, levelled his gun-hand across the broad tree trunk and opened fire.

Three of Mel's quick-fire bullets ripped close above the heads of the men's horses, causing them to buck and rear. The riders fought to regain control, as they brought their own guns to bear as Mel ran from cover.

Beckman wheeled his terrified cow pony about. He cut it into a run and rode the top of the slope. His companion, slower to move, saw Mel too, and after firing off a shot whipped his horse the other way.

Mel scrambled up the slope then weaved around some felled perimeter trees. He saw Beckman riding into a long, narrow wash. The other rider was already moving through boot-high grass on the far side. He pushed his gun into his pants top and carefully wiped the sweat and root dirt from his hands, waiting for the two men to ride from sight.

The attack had been carelessly planned, and that confused and worried Mel. He was sure Miner would have come after him himself and would probably have brought more backing than Beckman and another cowhand.

Mel ejected the spent cartridges from his revolver and refilled the cylinder from a handful of bullets he kept in his pocket. Then he turned and made his way back to the fruit grove. He was approaching the back of the house when he saw a rider coming fast along the wagon road. He broke into another run, then ran faster when he recognized the red, meaty face of Budge Miner.

Miner saw Mel, too, and wheeled his horse off the track. He rode straight at Mel, his eyes vengeful. But Mel had outguessed him in time. A desperate, head-long dash for the cover of the water trough along the side wall of the house gave Mel an advantage.

Miner had drawn his gun. He fired, fast and indis-criminately. The bullets cracked into the trough and whined off the pump head Mel had just repaired.

Mel swore as he hit the ground. He rolled, raised himself on his elbows and loosed off two shots in return. Wet dirt spat up into his face and he lay down again, rubbing at his eyes with the sleeve of his shirt.

'I'm getting real sick and tired of you, Miner,' he yelled, getting to his feet. He stood with his back to the wall and brought up his Colt. Just before Miner swung his horse's head away, Mel fired.

The shot was calculated, the only one he had time to make. It missed. Bent low in the saddle, the Spool foreman was away. Mel stretched out and watched the man ride away. He couldn't pull the trigger for fear of hitting the horse, and he'd never do that. Mel walked toward the fleeing figure, fired one ill-omened shot into the air.

When Miner was out of range he stopped at the edge of the timber. He looked back for a moment, then, lashing his horse's gleaming shoulders, he raced away.

Mel plunged his head into the trough, shuddered and then gulped down the fresh, cool water. Then he rubbed his hands up his face into his hair. As he walked to the front of the house he took the remaining bullets from his pocket and gripped them in his fist. 'One of these is for you, Miner, you son-of-a-bitch.'

There was deep silence now. Even the geese had found sanctuary under the floor timbers of the house. From near the front door Mel called out, 'Miss Church.'

With no immediate answer he called again, 'Miss Church . . . ma'am,' tentatively added, 'Reba,' then waited a long minute before he heard her telling him to go away.

'OK, if that's what you want,' he said, relieved that she wasn't hurt. 'An' don't go worrying about them visitors. It's over now.' After a few seconds more he added, 'They won't be coming back.'

Then he turned and walked across to the barn. Five minutes later he came back out, wearing his black coat with his Cree sash around his waist. He led his horse out into the yard, climbed slowly into the saddle.

From a front window Reba watched him nervously. But there was a difference now, and she felt a pang of shame. He'd stood resolute for her, on her land and faced the bullets that were fired point-blank at him.

She saw him ride from the yard, away beyond the barn. She went quickly to the door, and lifted out the security rail. She stepped out onto the veranda and waved her hand.

'Mr Cody. I'm sorry, I am all right,' she called, and listened to the empty echo of her words.

15

Mel rode down to the creek and made straight for the Spool ranchlands. In the past two days he'd traversed a sizeable section of the Church place, had discovered that Selwyn's fencing abutted not only fertile Spool land but vast tracts of desolate scrub. He cut through a section of fence and, with his hat pulled down hard over his eyes, headed west across the Spool wasteland. He saw tickseed and mallow – drylands plants not fit for graze – and better understood Spool's drive to gain old Selwyn's access to fresh, sweet water.

As he rode, his mind kept going back to the attack on the ranch, and to Reba Church. He wondered, worried that he should have remained, just in case the Spool men returned. But after a while, a slight, dawning smile broke across his face.

Yeah, that was it.

Exactly what he was supposed to think? Miner

carried a rifle and could have dropped him from a distance if he'd wanted to. The attack wasn't as carelessly planned as Mel had thought. The ploy was to draw fire, to keep him off the range.

He was riding along a low, stony ridge that rose into higher country when he reined in. To the south, he sighted dust rising above a long finger of pine that ran down from the main timber. He headed off, deeper into Spool country, pushing the grey for a few more miles until the terrain evened out.

The land spread out in big, gently rising slopes. Now he could see the dust again, closer and more clearly. He saw the slow-moving, patchy carpet, the bobbing brown heads of longhorns. It looked like four riders driving the herd, but the trail dust was thick and he was still too far away to be sure. He sat awhile and watched the advance of the herd, wondered why Spool was moving cattle through the crushing heat of the day.

Mel finally drew back and rode to the other side of the ridge. He swung down into a shallow valley, following a fence until it came to a run of the creek. He crossed in the shallows, and let the grey slurp some water before taking a run at the far slope. Within minutes he was looking down into another long trough of country, only this time it was well grassed. A collection of buildings spread midway along its northern aspect.

'Casper Spool,' Mel said aloud. 'That's just got to be you.'

He found a scrub pine and climbed from his horse. With his back against the bole of the tree he hunkered down, and built himself a smoke. From the ranch, he'd be silhouetted against the skyline, would have been an easy see for a lookout. He expected somebody to ride out to meet him with a rifle, but no one came.

Twenty minutes later, Mel was less than a quarter mile from the sandy yard that fronted the main ranch house. Only then did he notice movement from along the columned terrace of the two-storey building. The rest of the vast spread appeared to be deserted. He walked the grey steadily beneath a timbered archway, picking out the lone figure standing deep within the shade of the house's upper balcony.

When he was thirty yards from the porch rail, Casper Spool stepped forward and levelled a big Spencer rifle on him. But, coolly, Mel held his course and allowed the grey to keep going.

Spool moved a step sideways to position himself alongside one of the columns. 'That's far enough, mister. You've not been invited in,' he rasped.

Mel let his horse walk a few more paces into the slanting shade before he drew rein.

'You need some iron to ride in here,' Spool said.

'Why? I've done nothing wrong by you, have I?'

'Well, Miner doesn't think like that. He could be

here, just busting to strip your hide,' Spool suggested.

'I don't think so, Mr Spool. Anyway, I rode down here to talk to you . . . I need to ask you something,' Mel said.

'Ha. You decided to light out? You and that interfering McLane going to let the girl sell up as she pleases?'

Mel shook his head. 'No. No such luck.'

'What is it, then? What do you want?'

'Well, I'm learning, Mr Spool. I'm curious to know why a smart rancher would herd cattle in this heat.'

Spool regarded him suspiciously. 'What the hell are you talking about? What cattle . . . where?' he asked.

'Back a-ways. They're being pushed through that bad land of yours. I never got close enough to check the brand, but they certainly ain't Church stock.'

'A herd?' Spool asked incredulously.

'Yeah, an' running fast enough to lose most of their lard. Must be pushing three hundred head. That's a herd, ain't it?' Mel looked around him, then asked. 'It's sure quiet here. Your men out taking . . . some sort of picnic in the badlands?'

'What's that got to do with you? Did you come riding out here to cause trouble, Cody?'

Mel shook his head. 'No, why would I do that? Having you for a neighbour don't concern me much either way. But just a couple of hours back, Miner an'

Beckman an' another of your rabble paid the Church place a visit. Miner fired off some shots . . . came real close to nailing me. Now *that* concerns me, Spool. But you know – I got to thinking afterwards. What they was really trying to do was to make me stick real close to the ranch house. Close to Miss Church's skirts, if you get my meaning?'

Spool was plainly confused. He took a step toward the porch steps, held the rifle barrel across the terrace railings. 'What the hell are you gnawing at, Cody?'

'As far as I know about this country, there's no other ranches this side of Dog Creek. So those men I saw could be . . . probably are your hands . . . driving your cattle. That's what they never wanted me to see.'

Spool's mouth twisted into a sneer. 'My men are checking the fences, cleaning out Copper's tank ready for next month's drive. That's what they're doing.'

'No, they ain't. Come take a ride, we'll see who's right,' Mel suggested.

'Go to hell.'

'Given time I might well do that. But right now you're coming with me, Spool. I got a claim in this trouble.'

'You've got a claim? What the hell's it got to do with you anyway, whether my cattle are being herded or not?' Spool demanded.

'I think it was old Selwyn Church telling me that

130

he never stole cattle . . . never. But the truth didn't stop one of your men shooting him dead. That's one reason.' Mel's voice hardened as he continued. 'Then, of course, there's your ramrod. I ain't going to sleep too well at night just knowing he's out there somewhere. Maybe he got himself a dose of buck fever today, so I'd like to give him another chance. Beckman can buy in, an' maybe a couple of the others, if they feel that loyal to him.'

'You think you're that good, cowboy?'

After a fast, almost imperceptible movement of his right hand, Mel held his Colt, the barrel pointed straight at Spool's broad chest.

'I think maybe I'm good enough,' he advised with a thin smile. 'Right now, if you pull the trigger of that Spencer, we'll both die. So you got to ask yourself, is it worth it, Spool? Looking around, you got a hell of a lot more to lose than me.'

Spool didn't appear to be bothered by Mel's take on the situation, although he dropped the rifle barrel. 'These men?' he asked. 'Which way are they headed?'

'West. An' the longer we stand here pow-wowing the further we'll have to ride. If we lose the sun it won't be any easier travelling in that country . . . even for an *Injun* 'breed.'

Spool's breath was heavy. 'I'll get me a horse. By hell, Cody, we'll have ourselves a powder-burning contest if you're wrong,' he growled.

'Concern yourself with what'll happen if I'm right,' Mel said, calmly pushing his gun back into his sash.

16

Mel turned his horse from the yard and Spool followed. Together they rode off the home pastures and headed west.

Mel took the lead, and for two hours worked his way into the bare country. The deep red light of the setting sun was slanting into their eyes when they first found the lifeless, crushed ground of the drive.

'What the hell's going on?' Spool said. 'There's no cattle on this side of the range other than Church's stock, and those blackjacks couldn't make it across Dog Creek, let alone to Yuma.'

'You want we should go back?' Mel asked.

'Hell no,' Spool barked and heeled his horse forward.

They travelled another ten miles before Mel pointed ahead. The herd was settled, heads down around a cluster of hog wallows. Five men were riding close, giving the cattle a lick of water before taking advantage of the rustler's moon, pushing on through the night.

Spool dragged his big rifle from its scabbard, but Mel blocked the other horse with his grey. 'We don't know who we're shooting at,' he said. 'Best wait for morning. The rising sun'll give us the edge we need. Meantime you can decide what you're going to do.'

'What *I'm* going to do?'

'Yeah. I figure they're your cattle.' Mel swung down from his horse. He stretched out on the warm ground, pulled his hat over his eyes.

Spool slapped the barrel of his big rifle against his leg. 'You figure to sleep, with them owl hoots making off with the herd?'

'*Your* herd!' Mel snapped back. 'I'll hear 'em when they move out, which won't be long. For the minute, I ain't going nowhere. I've been doing work I ain't rightly used to . . . got aches in muscles I never knew I had.'

Spool got down from his horse, let it mouth a tuft of cheat grass. 'What work's that, Cody?'

'Fixing up the Church place. She's going to stay, you know . . . Miss Reba. She's like one of them Red River boats . . . got an oak keel, probably some of her uncle's stubbornness too.' Mel lifted his hat away from his face, looked up at Spool. 'What was your bellyache with old Selwyn? Must've been something besides creek water?'

Spool thought for a moment before he answered.

'He left his fences to rot. His longhorns strayed onto my place an' mixed with my Herefords. He should've been more careful ... should've moved on, but instead he hung on, stubborn as a mule.'

'And that's why you branded him a cattle thief? Sent four of your men into town to beat up on him and kill him?'

'No, I never did that,' Spool railed, not liking Mel's charge. 'I've never sent anyone to do my work, Cody. Not that sort of work. Not so long ago I fought to keep every goddamn blade of grass. There was hardly a man for hire you could trust, and I saw off nesters and sheep men. I had to drive cattle all the way to Mexico to get me a fair deal. No, mister, I never needed to send men to do my work.'

Mel kept quiet. It was as close as he could get to letting Spool know he believed him without saying so.

Spool stared out to where the herd was still watering. He rubbed the grey stubble of his chin, kicked each foot as if trying to move trapped grit around. 'It looks like they're getting ready to move them out,' he said.

He went to his horse and Mel did the same. For the next few hours they rode beyond the herd's dust, pushing further west across the hostile, darkening country.

'Hold up,' Mel called. He cut his horse across Spool's

track, and the rancher drew rein.

'What is it?' Spool asked.

'There's Copa Gully up ahead. If we ride the higher ground we'll be looking down on 'em. Should be close enough for you to let me know if they're your riders.'

Already the early light was good enough for Spool to see a mile ahead. But a thick cloud of yellow dust hung as a screen between him and the slow-moving herd, forcing him to ride with a neckcloth pulled high around his face.

Mel was working his way up a long, sloping trail, and Spool reluctantly decided to follow him. They rode steadily higher for close to another hour, and then, with the sun beginning its long, daytime burn, they reached a plateau that flattened off beyond the gully.

Mel stopped there and climbed from the saddle. 'We've got ahead of 'em,' he said. 'They got to come through here, but they won't see us. We'll wait up.'

Spool compassed the country about him, then he hitched his horse back out of sight. He brought the Spencer and flattened himself on the ground beside Mel.

'By hell, if you are right about Miner, I want the treacherous dog all for myself,' he said. 'You hear me, Cody? He's mine.'

Mel shrugged. 'It'll be him that's going to make the play. An' when he does, I won't be waiting for you to take over. Sorry, Spool.'

Spool studied him grimly for a moment but said nothing. Below them, the lead cattle were already moving into the head of the gully with the remainder of the herd in straggled lines behind. The five riders were bunched close, as if their lives were to be saved that way.

Mel lifted a hand and shaded his eyes. 'Can you make 'em out yet?' he asked.

'I can't see a goddamn thing,' Spool complained.

'Yeah. We'll see better when they're below us. We won't be looking into the light,' Mel said.

They waited while the hot sun got higher, powered down onto their backs. A breeze drifted up into their faces, but it carried hot, peppery dust from the desert floor.

Slowly the herd came on. Spool continually rebuked one and all as he waited for the riders to move up close enough for naming. When the untidy spread began to bunch up directly below them, Spool raised himself to get a better view. Mel knew that anybody looking up couldn't see them against the high sun, and kneeled alongside him.

Spool hissed a curse as he pointed down to the first rider. 'Miles Beckman,' he growled. 'And Felix Chelloe, damn his hide. I never did like the look of him. His eyes are set too close together.'

Mel was smiling to himself as Spool jumped to his

feet. The rancher hurried for his horse and was in the saddle before Mel had fully considered the situation. Mel shook his head, walked to his grey and gave chase. He wasn't overly concerned, even relieved that Spool took the trail that would bring him out at the head of the herd.

Spool had drawn fifty yards clear by the time Mel reached the bottom of the sloping trail. When Spool sensed he was caught, he slowed his horse to a trot. 'This is my fight. They're my cattle, my men and they're on my land.'

Mel drew alongside the fierce rancher. 'I don't care a goddamn spit in hell about any of that, Spool. But no one's firing a gun at me because I made it easy, you hear?'

Spool cursed and swallowed his angry words. 'OK, we let the herd go by,' he snapped out. 'But then I'm going for 'em. You got that?'

Even as they spoke, Mel was working his way across the gully. The lead steers trod wearily between them, tossing their heads uneasily as they continued. The bulk of the herd then crowded mindlessly past in their wake.

Shielded by an outcropping, Mel sat his horse. Across from him, Spool, too, sat hunched forward in the saddle. He was seething with fury, peering into the low pall of dust and trying to stifle a thick cough.

Mel was looking for the last of the herd when he saw Spool kick his horse away from the gully wall. As the dust thinned he saw the old rancher riding straight for the drovers. The Spool men were all riding drag, picking up stragglers, when through the rolling carpet of dirt they saw their boss, Casper Spool, bearing down on them.

17

Miles Beckman shouted a warning. He wheeled his horse about and the others drew rein, staring ahead, unbelieving.

'Yeah, it's me, the one who pays you, you thieving scum. Prepare yourselves,' Casper Spool yelled. Anger had got the better of him and he pulled a big Colt from his holster and took the centre ground, throwing shots ahead of him as he raced forward.

The stunned riders broke apart at Spool's wild offensive. Beckman swerved for a wall of the gully when he saw Mel Cody charging toward him and he fired. The gun roared in the steep rocky confines, the bullet slicing across Mel's left arm.

Mel issued a comforting word to his grey, and reined the horse 'til its flanks brushed the walls of the gully. He gritted his teeth and brought his Colt to bear on Beckman. The injury to his arm was bloody but slight. He recalled his father's words about being caught in a gunfight.

You've maybe learned about one trusty bullet being enough if right's on your side? Well, forget it, son. Go for the belly, an' put in three.

Two of Mel's bullets hit Beckman. One of them smashed into the man's side as he tried to swing his horse away. The other hit below his ear as he jerked forward in the saddle.

As its rider took the bullets, Beckman's horse whirled about and threw up its forelegs in an attempt to scale the gully walls. Then it slammed its hoofs back into the ground, and Beckman was pitched from the saddle. His body spread eagled into the gully floor. Dust fell, and immediately crusted the broken flesh of his face. His horse squealed its terror and took wild flight.

Spool saw the shooting and cursed violently. He looked about as Felix Chelloe's bullet thumped into his upper leg. He groaned with the searing stab of pain, but he was a wronged man in a rage, and too hardy to falter. As Chelloe thundered toward him, he reined in, threw his handgun to the ground and pulled the Spencer rifle. He lifted the big gun over the shoulder of his horse and fired point-blank range at the cowhand.

'Meet your maker, boy,' he rasped.

Chelloe threw up his arms as the flat-nosed .52 bullet exploded into his chest. He went backwards and sideways, with one foot remaining trapped in its

141

stirrup. Like Beckman's, his horse veered away in panic, heading back toward the end of the gully. Mel watched in heart-thumping disgust as the horse sped by, Chelloe's lifeless body rolling, leaving a twisting, thin trail of bloodied dust.

Mel patted his grey's neck and looked back to where the drover had ridden from. The other three riders had withdrawn. They were sitting their horses with their hands spread and away from their holstered guns.

He rode slowly down the gully to confront them. His eyes were wary, and he rested his gun-hand across the horn of his saddle. Just ahead of him, Spool was moving too. The rancher was hurt and visibly shaken. He'd come too close to being killed by his own men.

'Don't know what in tarnation's going on here, Mr Spool, but we been taking orders,' one of the drovers spoke up hastily.

'Taking orders from who?' Spool demanded.

'Budge Miner. He said to get the herd onto the barrens through Copa Gully,' the man said anxiously. 'We didn't figure it was right, Mr Spool. Me nor the boys here, an' that's the truth.'

'It's a goddamn tale to keep me from stringing you up,' Spool rasped. 'What's your name, mister?'

'Jake Tanner,' the man said. 'We was hired by Miner a week ago.'

Spool had a severe look at the two other men.

'Miner told us there was work if we wanted it.

142

Never planned to rob the big house,' Tanner said.

Spool glowered at him. 'Another likely damn yarn,' he said.

'Ain't no yarn, Mr Spool. We never took from no one,' said another man.

'I'll remember you said that, mister,' Spool threatened.

'You can check our guns, they're cold. Anyhow, they'd probably blow up in our faces if we used 'em,' the man offered as a further defence.

Mel reached out a hand to Tanner. The gun resembled Mel's own Colt, but was a cheap imitation of the real thing, making a harsh grating noise when he spun the cylinder. 'Leave 'em be, Spool,' he said. 'It's Miner we both want.'

Tanner pointed back along the trail. 'He pulled back, mid-afternoon. Said he was going to check with Mr Spool about pushing the herd through the night. He should have been back by now.'

Mel worked his horse closer, looked at the doubtful Spool. 'We're wasting time. Their story sits well with me.'

Tanner tipped the brim of his hat and nodded obligingly. Then he looked straight at Spool. 'Them cattle of yours'll be running 'emselves to bone,' he said. 'We best get after 'em . . . turn 'em back to pasture. What do you say, Mr Spool?'

Spool rubbed a gnarled hand across his face, looked back through the gully. 'What about

Beckman and Chelloe? You going to take care of them too?'

'If we don't, them buzzards will,' Tanner said, inclining his head to the clear blue sky.

A malevolent grin crossed Spool's face. 'They're circling on an ill wind, sure enough.'

'I'm interested in where you made the pick-up,' Mel said to Tanner.

'They were corralled on land beyond the creek. They been there for a couple of days,' Tanner told him.

'Church's land,' Mel confirmed. He'd not ridden that far in his exploration yet. If not for Miner's strike at the ranch, he'd have stumbled on the herd soon enough and known that trouble was in the wind.

'My cattle on Church land,' Spool said quietly, as if to himself.

'They're still running, Mr Spool,' Tanner went on. He'd slowly lowered his hands, was twitching his reins.

Spool thought for a moment, looked hard at the riders. 'OK, go get 'em,' he ordered. 'We'll talk everything out later.'

Tanner and the other two turned their mounts and rode off. Mel sat his horse, flexed his fingers as the sting in his arm spread to his hand.

'You been elected? 'Cause you're sure losing a mess of blood,' he said, seeing the dark wet spread down

Spool's leg.

'I've been nominated, that's all. I'll live.'

'Looks like Selwyn didn't die for nothing,' Mel said tellingly.

'Looks like it,' Spool accepted. 'One day maybe I'll get to thank him. In the meantime, I'll just burn me a deeper brand into Miner's hide.'

'Maybe Reba Church would like to hear something from you,' Mel suggested.

'Don't get me wrong, Cody, I'm not rolling over. That land business isn't finished yet. I'm still aiming to get the girl to sell up. What's more, I'm not paying you any respect for today's work.'

'That's all right, Spool. I weren't looking for any,' Mel retorted.

Spool grimaced, then swore. 'I got to get back to the ranch. Get this goddamn leg seen to.'

'Yeah, you do that,' Mel said and hauled away.

As he rode south, Mel went over the past few days in his mind. None of what had happened mattered much to him, except Selwyn dying. After a while he climbed from the saddle, walked the grey a mile or so. Then he remounted and ran the horse toward where Reba Church would be.

18

Budge Miner reached the Spool ranch at first dark. Finding the other hands had eaten and retired to the bunkhouse, he walked across the yard and knocked on the big, white-painted door of the main house.

Miner wanted to stall, needing time for Beckman and Chelloe to get the cattle off Spool's land. He intended to spend most of the night jawing with his boss, while the herd got close to the sale pens outside Yuma. When there was no response to his knock, he turned the great latch ring and pushed open the door. He called Spool's name, then, slightly troubled at the quiet, he stepped back onto the terrace.

After thinking about it for a moment, he decided Spool had likely gone to town, but he was worried. The Spool ramrod sauntered back across the yard to the bunkhouse where some of the itinerant cowboys were playing blackjack.

'Anybody seen Mr Spool?'

The men shook their heads without looking up. But Otto Ribb, a long-time hand, raised his eyes. 'Maybe he's gone to town. What's up?'

'Seems there's a lot of help missing. Beckman, Chelloe and Tanner . . . one or two others that were working the bottom slopes. They should all have been back by now.'

Ribb sniffed derisively. 'Happen they run across that 'breed, that hair-lifter we heard so much about. People round here get real skittish when his name's mentioned. 'Cody', ain't it . . . his white man's name? Seems he goes on the warpath when he's put out any.'

'You don't know what you're talking about, Ribb,' Miner snapped. 'Just get yourself ready for tomorrow. You'll likely be riding all day.' Knowing something had gone wrong, Miner angrily left the bunkhouse. He was uneasy as he saddled up a fresh horse.

As he rode, he was hoping that Spool had either gone to town or was paying the Church girl another visit. Either way, when the loss of the cattle was finally discovered, he hoped to have the herd money safely stashed and be riding back with Beckman and Chelloe.

For Casper Spool, Miner had his story all worked out. He'd tell how they'd trailed cattle thieves into the barren land, got ambushed in the gully, and lost three men as well as the herd. Maybe then, by using a crooked truth, he'd get some backup to take out the stumbling block called Mel Cody. Perhaps he'd call in on the Church girl himself, offer his deceitful commiserations and console her after having sold out to Spool.

He single-footed his horse west, into the night. There was no real hurry. He didn't much care about catching up with Beckman and the others, having to swallow trail dust for his trouble.

When he emerged from the timbered slopes, Miner almost crossed Casper Spool's way. He'd been escaping the full blast of the sun when he sighted the lone rider coming back from the direction of the gully.

At first he thought it was Beckman or one of the other hands riding back to meet up with him. But he drew back into the trees when he saw it was Spool who rode past.

Miner cursed. Spool was slumped forward, gripping the saddle-horn. Then he saw the dark blood, thickly congealed across and down the man's leg. Spool's face was haggard, but determined, and his eyes were set straight ahead.

Miner was unnerved. His mind raced, but he sat in the saddle very still. He watched the rancher until he was a long way past, half expecting him to fall heavily from his horse.

The old man was nearly a mile off before Miner decided to make a move. He kicked his own horse, spurring it fast across the open country. He was headed for the high ground that fell sharply down behind the Spool ranch house.

A good hour later he slipped from his horse and hitched it in the shade at the back of the spread. He walked cautiously around the outbuildings, then waited until he saw Spool making his way across the yard that fronted the big house.

Three men came running from assorted work sheds. They ran to Spool and helped him down from his horse, carried him toward the house and up the steps while Miner slunk quietly around to the back porch.

With his gun in his hand, Miner stood with his back hard-pressed against the rear wall of the house. He was breathing deeply and his heart thumped with the fear of what might have happened, the aftermath of Spool's misadventure.

From inside the house, he heard an excited voice.

'You going to tell us what happened, boss?' the old ranch-hand, Otto Ribb, was asking. 'You want me to send someone into town for the doc?'

'No, you see to it, Otto. It looks bad, but it ain't more'n a flesh wound. It's Miner I want. Where is he?' he asked savagely.

'He was here, asking the same of you, boss. Not more than a few hours ago.'

Miner gripped the butt of his gun until his hand shook. He realized that Spool had caught up with the stolen herd; that's where he'd got his wounds from. And he must have spoken at some time with one of his riders, if not Beckman or Chelloe. But now Miner didn't know what state the herd was in, whether it had been pushed onto the Yuma cattle pens or not. Then he recalled that he'd only hired Jake Tanner and two other men to drive cattle. They weren't in on the deal. He was in a mess, and knowing he had to stay and find out more, he cursed his luck.

'Cody came through here. I think he was looking for Miner,' Spool shouted angrily. 'Told me about a herd being pushed Yuma way. So together, we went down to have a look. We found Beckman an' Chelloe all right. They had three new hands with 'em . . . driving my cattle through Copa Gully. Cody an' me, we just rode into the point, shot 'em dead.'

Miner heard the startled voices of disbelief. He cursed and hissed for them to keep quiet, waited for the silence to settle again.

'An' that ain't the best part of it,' Spool went on. 'One of them others, Tanner, said it was *Miner's* plan they were hired to work to.'

'What you want us to do, boss?' Ribb asked.

'Get out an' help bring back them beeves. But not you, Otto. You got to help patch me up. Tie me to my saddle if you have to.'

'You going after Miner, boss?'

'Yeah. An' it'll be a lot more'n that when I've figured out where he's gone.'

Miner felt the cold shiver between his shoulder blades. He was about to back off when he heard Chick.

'What about him off the reservation . . . Mel Cody? Who's he riding with then, boss?' the man asked.

'Well, he ain't with us. But then again, he ain't against us, either. You men steer clear of him, you hear? I'll handle him when the time comes.'

Miner didn't wait to hear more. He fast-tracked back to his horse and heeled away up the slope. Frustration and anger burned through him now. His scheme was in ruins, and mostly due to the intervention of the 'breed called Mel Cody. He checked the cylinder of his Colt and, headed for Church country.

19

Reba Church heard the alarmed honking of the geese and rose, startled, from where she'd been sitting half-asleep on the porch. She looked out at the yard and home pasture for sign of a horse, but saw none, and realized the sounds were from the back of the house. Perturbed, she reached for the door latch, but it suddenly opened away from her, catching her off-balance.

'Mister Cody? Mel?' But the words died in her throat when she saw Budge Miner standing in the shadows of her main room.

The man's face was pouring with sweat, still blotched and ugly from his encounter with Mel. Reba couldn't help thinking of a giant slice of pan-fried chicken and she drew back in silent horror, her body tense.

Miner stepped quickly forward and grabbed her wrist. 'No, it ain't him,' he sneered. 'Ain't that just too bad? Or maybe not, eh, pretty miss?'

'Get off me!' Reba shouted, but Miner pulled her close. She smelled his hot, muggy odour and clawed his face. He cursed and dragged her further into the house. Reba kicked out, but Miner's strength was too much. He hurled her down onto the couch.

'You little wolverine,' he said, holding his fingers to the side of his face.

'Get out of my house!' Reba screamed, her mind flying through defences and escapes.

'Shut your mouth,' Miner told her. 'You make another sound like that an' I'll mark you. I'll cut you so's your 'breed friend won't recognize you when he gets here.'

All colour drained from Reba's face and she started to tremble uncontrollably. All she could think of was Mel Cody.

Miner wiped blood across his face, onto his chin. 'Seems you get yourself a front-row seat when me an' him meet,' he snarled. 'Only this time the ending's going to be different, eh, missy?'

Reba leaped to her feet and raced for the door. But Miner had seen it coming and was too quick. He placed himself in the doorway and as she lunged at him he gave a dead-bone grin.

'Yeah that's it, missy,' he said. 'A man like me can take that an' more.'

Reba lashed out with her foot and caught him low in the leg. Miner threw a punch at her head and she felt the hard, dark thud. Then she felt herself being grabbed, lifted bodily from the floor. There was a wild rush of air, then a smack of pain across her body.

Miner walked over to where he'd thrown her. He grabbed her by the hair and pulled her to her feet. He ripped the top of her blouse from her shoulders while Reba clawed at his face. She tore open his bottom lip and Miner smashed her down to the floor again.

Reba tried to rise, to stay awake and warn Mel. But her hands gripped at nothing and she collapsed with her cheek against the floorboards she'd so recently scrubbed. She sobbed just once, then lost her senses as the painful dark enveloped her.

Mel Cody rode into the yard of the Church ranch at mid-afternoon. The whole place was quiet, and from the moment he'd started down the grassy slope, he'd felt an uneasy tension gripping his vitals. The geese were nipping at long grass in the orchard and there was no sign of Reba.

He watched the house closely, half expecting her to come out and greet him, curious to know what had happened. As he rode toward the house, he rehearsed just how he'd tell her how he'd resolved the trouble with her neighbour, Casper Spool.

He reined in at the hitch rail, but remained saddled. He lashed out with his boot as the geese came running and swore he'd kill them if Miner didn't get him first. Then he rolled stiffly from his horse, dropped the reins as he saw movement from behind the front window. He had only taken one step towards the stable when the window shutter was smashed open and a gun roared at him.

Mel felt the warm pulse of air as the bullet missed his left eye. He dropped to a crouch but held his fire, uncertain of Reba's whereabouts.

The gun roared again. This time the shot smashed his left shoulder and sent him twisting to the ground. 'Miner,' he said as he rolled with the impact. Another bullet came, spitting the hard-packed yard dirt into his face. He continued to roll, seeking shelter below the low, planked veranda of the house. Each turn sent pain stabbing deep into his chest, up into his neck.

When he got to the relative safety of the corner of the house he got to his feet. His left arm was already unusable, his left hand rigid with pain. He worked his way down the side of the house to the water trough. Then he heard the clump of boot steps from inside, as another bullet tore through the small side window. He grinned, mumbled, 'Stupid, he's going to kill you,' and doubled over.

He went on and turned across the rear of the house. He banged on the door, ran faster right the way around the building, until he came to the front corner. He took six quiet steps to the front door and stopped for a moment. Then he pushed his Colt back into his waistband, and called on his forebears for strength as he lifted the latch.

As he hoped, Miner was coming through the house from the back, where he'd heard Mel bang on the door. He fired on instinct, but Mel leaped to the side, throwing himself to the floor as he came in. Through the instant tear of pain, he saw Reba. She was looking at him. He held out his right hand, hoping she'd stay down.

But she was still dazed. She looked at him with scared, confused eyes. Mel could see the distress and a grimace bent his features.

He stepped up and looked toward Miner, grimaced when he saw the bloody mess of the man's face. He stood very still, dared Miner to fire because he'd been counting. But the closeness of certain death for one of them was too much for Miner and a final, desperate bullet buried itself in the wall planks behind him.

'Stay down!' Mel yelled at Reba while staring into Miner's eyes. He'd got it right – Miner had to reload.

Mel felt like apologizing for using the advantage of thinking. Instead, he drew the Colt from his waistband with his right hand and with a cheerless shake of his head, steadied himself and fired. The first shot ripped low into Miner's neck, the second and third into his chest and belly. The man's legs buckled and he went down.

Miner was a big man and had a few moments of

life left in him. He gurgled a curse and held his shattered neck with one hand, swung his gun up with the other. The empty chambers made their dull, empty clicks. He dropped the gun and raised his arm, twisting his fingers into the fabric of Reba's newly tacked-up curtains.

Reba looked at the still-smoking gun in Mel's hand as she started to raise herself from the floor. With one arm, Mel clumsily helped her to her feet and noticed the dark bruise high on the side of her face.

'I'm gonna need a moment,' she said with a tight smile.

'Yeah, you an' me both,' he returned.

He pushed the Colt back into his waistband and pulled off his coat, then blinked at the pain of his bloodied arm and shoulder. He turned away from Reba as he roughly twisted his shirtsleeve tight around the wound. The searing pain made him curse long and loud as he dragged the heavy body across the yard. But he didn't stop until he'd made the ground between the fruit trees. He let go his grip of Miner's sweat-stained collar and watched the man's meaty face press deep into the grass.

'Eat goddamn worms, you son-of-a-bitch,' he said coldly.

Back in the house, the cloying heat and cordite fumes almost overcame him. He looked at his shoulder and his arm, ground his teeth with the pain. But now Reba saw the blood running to his fingers, and was already on her feet.

'Outside on the rocker,' she said curtly. 'Now I'm fully rested, I'll take control.'

Twenty minutes later, after finishing the last of his forty-rod, Mel closed his eyes as Reba administered warm water, salve and a bandage.

'The bullet might still be in there,' she said. 'We'll have to get you into town, first thing. Doc McLane needs to see these wounds.'

But Mel's mind was elsewhere. 'I had a little animal once . . . never knew what it was. I kept it in a box,' he said ruefully. 'When it died, I poked it down a hole in the riverbank.'

'With one hand, you're going to poke that giant down a hole?' Reba asked in disbelief.

'No, not really. I thought about it, though. When Casper Spool gets here, as he surely will, he's going to feel real cheated when he finds Miner's body. So I'll leave the burying to him. A gesture of my good will.'

'Well, I'm glad I won't be here to see it,' Reba said.

'You're going? Leaving the ranch? But I thought—'

'Then you thought wrong . . . like me,' she interjected. 'I loathe just about everything there is in Polvo Gris. Mr Spool is welcome to all of it. Right now his money is as good as anyone else's.'

Mel had himself a few moments of thought before he spoke. 'I've had a look around, like my pa told me, an' he was right. But he only spoke about the richness of the land, not about those who own it.' Mel relaxed a little as the salve began its work. 'On the way down here from the north, I rode through Montana ... along the Yellowstone. There's a lot of free country, Reba, an' not much in the way of killing. So perhaps now I'll try there. It looked like somewhere my ma would have spoke well of.'

Reba looked Mel in the eye. 'Sounds almost too good to be true. Perhaps I'll leave everyone a forwarding address for somewhere along the Yellowstone. What do you think?'

Mel opened one eye, nodded diffidently. 'I think you'd be real good company, ma'am ... real good,' he said quietly.

'Well, that is good, then,' Reba declared with a smile. 'But right now, there's no rush to go anywhere. So perhaps you'd like something to eat? I can't go as far as asking what you'd really like, though. We don't have that much.'

While he thought of an answer, Mel untied his sash. With one hand, he wrapped it around his Colt, and tossed the bundle across the veranda. 'Oh there's enough,' he said, with a slow, wicked grin. 'I've had both them murderous geese plucked an' filled with apples. All you got to do is wring their necks an' cook 'em.'

Reba didn't move for a moment, or create much

159

of an expression. Then a smile broke across her face and she wagged a reproving finger as she grasped the joke.